Sherlock Holmes
and the
Frightened Golfer

Sherlock Holmes
and the
Frightened Golfer

J M Gregson

**BREESE
BOOKS
LONDON**

First published in 1999 by
Breese Books Ltd
164 Kensington Park Road, London W11 2ER, England

Reprinted February 2000

Front cover photograph is reproduced by kind permission of
Retrograph Archive

ISBN: 0 947 533 63 X

Typeset in 11½/14pt Caslon by
Ann Buchan (Typesetters), Middlesex
Printed and bound in Great Britain by
Itchen Printers Limited, Southampton

ONE

As I dressed myself unhurriedly on that late February morning in 1896, it seemed to me a day to be cheerful. The fog which had hung over London for the last miserable week, making the short days seem little more than gloomy intervals between the long winter nights, had lifted at last, and a pale sun gleamed on the damp housetops as I looked out towards Euston station. For the first time, I was aware of the lengthening of the days as the calendar moved forward.

Mrs Hudson seemed to share my cheerfulness as she brought in my breakfast and I gave her good morning. 'I can particularly recommend the devilled kidneys this morning, Dr Watson,' she said. 'Though there's some people who just don't seem to notice what they're eating, and the trouble that's been taken over it!' She glanced darkly towards the hidden presence at the other end of our rooms.

Holmes had plainly eaten long before I arrived at the table: not a good sign, for it usually betokened a sleepless night and an ill humour in that sinuous but restless mind. I enjoyed a leisurely breakfast, choosing to ignore the clouds of smoke which seeped into my vision above the pages of *The Morning Post* at the far end of the room. Then my worst fears were realised. From Holmes's bedroom, there erupted the sound of his violin – he played like a demented Paganini, as he always did when the shroud of depression fell around him. Unfortunately he had not the skill of that celebrated practitioner, and his arpeggios threatened the pleasure of my toast and marmalade.

I finished my meal and went and sat on an armchair in our sitting-room. My friend registered my presence only with a scowl, but I refused to be intimidated. 'I see we have a fine bright morning at last. The sort that convinces one that spring cannot be far away after all.' I went over to the window, eased the sash up with some difficulty, and gestured with a lordly arm at the sun outside.

'You act as though you had produced the morning yourself,' said Holmes roughly. 'As for the spring, it will come when it is ready. Even someone as unobservant as you, Watson, must have noticed by now that the seasons in our British climate vary very little in their arrivals and departures. The snowdrops have been out in Regent's Park for seventeen days now. I'll wager that this morning's sun will see the crocus in flower by the end of the week, and I have no doubt that the earliest of the narcissi are already in bud and waiting for people like you to wax lyrical over their arrival. I have no doubt that they will bloom within a week of their time last year, or the ten years before that, for that matter. As a man with some pretensions towards science, you are surely aware that the monthly soil temperatures in our London parks vary by less than a degree from year to year.'

'Indeed, I think I may have read something to that effect – possibly in one of your botanical monographs. But I was not looking for a lecture on the elements, Holmes, but merely making a cheerful observation on what seems likely to be a splendid day after the gloom we have lately endured. The normal small talk which helps to make the world –'

'I do not deal in small talk, Watson, as you should know by now.'

It was true, I knew, but I was stung to defend myself against what sounded like an attack. 'Small talk is the preliminary to friendship, Holmes. You can scarcely –'

'I dare say you are right. I have few friends, and those few have to exercise a degree of toleration I scarcely possess myself. But on the whole I like it that way. That way I can be ready for the more remarkable aspects of life, which tend to offer themselves without warning. As they may be doing at this very moment, for all we know. Unless I am very much mistaken, that hansom cab has stopped at the door of 221B.'

As soon as he said this, I felt that he was right. I had heard the faint sound of a horse's hooves at the end of the street as I had wrested up the window, but I had scarcely registered that the sound had ceased until Holmes commented upon it. Now the horse's steps rang clear again as the cab moved away, and the muffled tones of Mrs Hudson in the hall told me that we had a visitor.

'A fit man, obviously, and one in a hurry. I fancy he has come here straight from some outdoor activity,' said Holmes, as the noise of the caller's approach became louder.

I glanced at my friend, who had been transformed from querulous curmudgeon to eager detective by the prospect of action. He was standing with his head a little on one side and inclined towards the door and the stairs beyond it, like a bird listening intently for the sounds of its prey. I looked rather than asked my question, for the visitor was almost at the door. Holmes waved it aside with an impatient gesture, though I knew that he would answer, knew indeed that he would have been piqued if I had not prompted him. 'The man is ascending our narrow stairs at a great rate, in what sound to me like stout shoes made for outdoor work. As he has obviously gone ahead of Mrs Hudson rather than allowing her to precede him as his guide, he is obviously impatient to be with us.'

An instant later, the heavy door of our apartment flew open and a large man stood in the doorway, blinking a little in the sudden light after the darkness of the stairs, but scarcely even breathing heavily after a climb which cost me quite an effort. A fit man, as my friend had said, and one patently in a hurry. I glanced down automatically at his shoes; they were of thick and durable leather, of the kind some of my friends wore for shooting on the moors of Yorkshire and the hills of Scotland. I registered from the corner of my eye a small smile on the aquiline features of the man who had forecast this footwear.

Mrs Hudson arrived some seconds behind our visitor, breathless and a little indignant at his lack of decorum. 'Gentleman to see you, Mr Holmes. I said I thought it would be in order, but Mr Bullimore thought there would be no need for me to check that.'

She stared at him resentfully as she struggled for breath after this announcement. Bullimore said with an apologetic smile and a good deal of charm, 'I'm sorry indeed, madam, if I have rushed through your house and inconvenienced you. Forgive me for being so precipitate. But the nature of my business with Mr Sherlock Holmes is indeed urgent.'

Holmes said with only the faintest trace of irony, 'That's all right, Mrs Hudson. Thank you for ensuring that our visitor was with us so promptly,' and our long-suffering landlady withdrew, mollified as easily as she always was by Holmes.

The man who had now come into the middle of the room thrust out his hand to each of us in turn. 'Alfred Bullimore. It may be that you are able to reassure me in due course. But it is also possible that I am in urgent need of your services, Mr Holmes.'

He spoke abruptly, so that one had the impression of joining a conversation in the middle rather than at the outset. A man who did not waste time on small talk. Holmes should take to him readily enough, I thought huffily. My friend stood motionless, with his head still a little on one side, weighing up our visitor without troubling to disguise the fact. Bullimore was a strongly built man of around six feet, wearing a russet Harris Tweed suit. He had thick brown hair, which was beginning to recede a little but carried no trace of grey. He had a wide moustache, waxed into points at the end in the fashion of the time, though one end had lost a little of its rigidity and curled slightly upwards, which gave his face a faintly comic look, despite his agitation.

Holmes said, 'We shall need to know a little of your background, sir, so that we may put your mission into its context. We deduce, of course, that you are a gentleman of some means, who spends much of his time outdoors. I notice that you take a modest pride in your own fitness and strength. Probably in your physical skills also, since I suspect you spend much of your time on one of the golf courses which seem to be springing up all around our overcrowded metropolis.'

Bullimore's firm jaw dropped. It was a moment I always found appealing, though I had seen it happen so often before and with so many of the great man's clients. 'How the devil do you know that? I sent no preliminary letter, and surely no one else can have acquainted you with the problem I have come here this morning to set before you.'

'A trifle, Mr Bullimore, nothing more. I am happy if my informed guess happens again to be right.'

Bullimore looked at me, still obviously suspecting some sort of trick. 'His informed guesses usually are right,' I said.

'And when they are not, my chronicler is charitable enough not to reproduce them,' said Holmes sardonically. 'You will have gathered by now that this is my esteemed friend Dr Watson, the man who has recorded some of my previous modest successes. A little melodramatically, to my mind, but accurately, I suppose, as far as the facts go.'

'Indeed I have read some of Dr Watson's admirable accounts of your cases. That is the main reason why I am here. But pray tell me how you seem to know so much of me already, Mr Holmes.'

'It is obvious enough, surely? Your attire is of the best quality, so you are clearly a man of means. But it is not a business dress: you have evidently not come here from business in the city, nor from one of the recognised professions. Your face has a ruddy health which argues a regular exposure to the elements, even through the harsh winter which is almost at an end now. Yet you have no tan, which argues you must spend much of your time outdoors in our own benighted climate. You are dressed for it, indeed, and so warmly and sensibly that you came here today without feeling the need to don an overcoat. That reinforces the impression of haste, of course. Watson and I had already remarked on your precipitate arrival and enthusiastic assault upon our staircase.'

Bullimore looked a little embarrassed. 'Yes. I do tend to go a little headlong at things, I suppose, once I've taken a decision. But look here, you said more than that, and I don't possibly see how –'

'Nothing, really. A detail I fastened upon as soon as you appeared in our doorway, Mr Bullimore. Your tweeds are of the sort normally adopted for golf, I think. And for several other outside activities as well, of course. But your jacket, whilst generally in good condition, is worn slightly, just a little bare, on the right shoulder. It is obvious to me at least that you have carried something on that shoulder to make such a mark, and I deduced a bag of golf sticks. Hence my thought that you are a man who feels fit enough to scorn physical assistance and prides himself upon his own fitness: you are a man who could obviously afford a caddie to carry your clubs around and tee up the ball for you if you wished it!'

Alfred Bullimore shook his head admiringly. 'It all sounds very simple when you explain it, and no doubt it is, to you.'

'Then may we move straight on to the reason for your presence here? It must be a matter of some urgency, since you have come here straight from the course.'

'It is. But how can you know that?'

'Nothing more than routine observation, Mr Bullimore. You could do it yourself. You have a splash of mud on your left toe cap, which is not yet dry, and a blade of grass in the welt of your shoe, which on a fine morning like this suggests that you have been abroad early, on damp turf. Moreover, there are grains of sand on the left calf of your trousers, which I expect come from the mounds of sand on which you tee your ball to drive. And your moustache, if you will forgive so personal a comment, has lost its wax at one side and thus its original symmetry. It is obvious that you have come straight from the course, without consulting even a mirror.'

Alfred Bullimore's hand flew automatically to the straying facial hair. His fingers twirled it back to its original rectitude. For a moment he looked a little discomforted; then he smiled and said, 'I see that very little escapes you, Mr Holmes. Dr Watson has in no way exaggerated your powers.'

Holmes shrugged. 'He has sensationalised them at times. In what he pleased to call *A Study in Scarlet* he transformed a routine investigation into an absurdly dramatic affair. But I suppose I must be grateful to him. His account has subsequently brought me some interesting work.'

'And you may regard what I bring to you today as another interesting problem. Though "alarming" is more the term I would choose myself.'

Holmes sighed. 'I am ready to listen, Mr Bullimore. But you have still not given me more of your background than I have deduced for myself. We have established that you are a golfer. But, by your clothes and your bearing, not one who is paid for his services.'

Bullimore smiled at the idea; he did not seem insulted by the notion that he might be one of the club repairers who were beginning to make a living from the game by establishing their own shops on the courses and playing for prize money. 'No, Mr Holmes. I am an enthusiast for the game – indeed, some of my friends say that I am almost a fanatic. But I have the means to indulge my passion as an amateur.'

There was a short, awkward silence. It was I who said, 'But surely that is not your only occupation, Mr Bullimore? Perhaps you have a calling which allows you a generous amount of leisure to indulge your passion for golf.'

'No, Dr Watson. I follow no occupation at present. No paid occupation, at any rate. I am the Secretary of Blackheath Golf Club, but that of course is an honorary post and carries no remuneration. I have a successful haberdashery business and a farm in Devon, but I take no part in the running of these enterprises. They are run by efficient managers and I never interfere.'

'So you do nothing but play golf?'

Perhaps the surprise I intended to conceal showed in my tone, for he looked me full in the face for a moment and I thought he was going to take offence. Then he laughed suddenly, in the abrupt manner that was already beginning to seem a characteristic of his, and said, 'That is correct. I know a man of your professional background would find such a life difficult to comprehend, but I have devoted myself to seeing just how far I can go in this infuriating game. I hope to challenge the very best, the professionals like Vardon and Taylor and Braid. I have watched them, many times, and they are good. But not so good that I feel that I cannot rival them, if I continue to work at my game.' His enthusiasm shone out of the weatherbeaten countenance. In the new century, we have become used to men regarding sport as worthy of their fullest energies and concentration, but it was in 1896 the first time that either I or my friend had met anyone who so unashamedly declared his devotion to a mere game.

It was Holmes who said brusquely, 'Well, Watson, it is a man of your profession, Dr Grace, who has set the example in making a sport the centre of his life. And I believe he has done very well out of it. But what is it that brings you here so hastily this morning, Mr Bullimore?'

'This, Mr Holmes.' Bullimore produced a sheet of paper from the pocket of his tweed jacket with a rather theatrical flourish and spread it upon the table for us to peruse.

BE WARNED BY WHAT HAS HAPPENED. IF YOU PERSIST IN YOUR DESIRE TO CARRY AWAY GOLF TROPHIES, YOU WILL NOT LONG SURVIVE IN THIS WORLD. DESIST NOW WHILST YOU ARE IN GOOD HEALTH, OR THE CONSEQUENCES WILL BE DEATH FOR YOU AND FOR OTHERS.

Holmes studied the paper for several moments without speaking, then looked equally intently into the face of the man who had brought it. 'A strange message, Mr Bullimore. Unpleasant, indeed, but perhaps no more than that. You do not look to me like a man easily disturbed by such nonsense. On its own, this could be the missive of a troublesome crank. Such men rarely carry out their extravagant threats; usually they have neither the means nor the will to do so. But I suspect you have more to tell us.'

'I have, sir. This is but the latest and most outrageous of a series of such messages.'

'And how have these communications been delivered?'

'Until this one, they came through the post. They were addressed to me as Secretary of Blackheath Golf Club.'

'Do you have them?'

No. I refused to take them seriously. My attitude was exactly the one you have just described. I have a contempt for anyone who is not prepared to put his name to a letter, and I considered them to be in any case no more than the outpourings of some deluded and unbalanced individual.'

'But you speak in the past tense. You no longer consider our mysterious correspondent to be harmless?'

'No. In the last month, there have been a series of incidents, involving damage to the property of our members. A gentleman was having lunch when his bag of clubs was removed and balls and sticks were spread around the eighteenth green. A week ago, two members had the shafts of most of their clubs smashed in two whilst they were in our locker room. Next, a set of clubs of my own was tossed upon a bonfire which our greenkeeper had lighted to dispose of fallen timber. Then, two nights ago, an elderly member was walking his small dog across the course when he was tripped and felled on the eighth hole, and his dog kicked so savagely that it had to be put down.'

I said, 'But that incident could surely be unconnected with the previous ones. A footpad or some other desperate villain might have been tempted to violence by the prospect of a victim who would offer little resistance.'

'That was my first thought. But Captain Osborne, the gentleman involved, was not robbed, though he carried almost ten pounds in his pockets and had a gold repeater watch which must have been worth much more than that. And I think the note I have brought you this morning carries a veiled reference to the incident in its first phrase: 'Be warned by what has happened.'

Holmes picked up the sheet of paper and examined it through his magnifying glass. 'A common enough brand of cheap writing paper, obtainable at any stationer's. And standard black ink, applied with a newish medium nib. Nothing much for us there.' He turned his attention to the letters of the message. 'The fellow – I shall assume for the moment that our culprit is male – has used capitals to remain anonymous, and he appears to have produced most of the straight strokes through the application of a ruler.'

'Perhaps his script and his utensils indicate that our man belongs to what Mr Keir Hardie now talks of as the working classes,' I ventured.

'Or that we have a man who is clever enough to suggest that hasty conclusion to us,' said Holmes loftily. Mr Bullimore, you have no doubt made some of your own enquiries into this business.'

'Yes. I took a cab and toured all the golf clubs in our area of London yesterday. None of them had endured any of the troubles we have had at Blackheath.'

'Then our man seems to be aiming his mischief at your members alone.'

'Worse than that, from my point of view. I believe the malice is personal. The messages I have received previously were all directed at me, as this one seems to be.'

'Hmm. It is a pity that you destroyed them. You say they came by post. Did you notice any of the post marks?'

'They were local. But then, everything points to this villain being somewhere in the vicinity. He knows the club. Knows my own movements, indeed. I have an uncomfortable feeling that I am being watched, on and off the golf course.'

'You say this latest message did not come by post. Where then did you receive it?'

'That's what I mean about feeling that this wretched man knows all about my routine,' said Bullimore grimly. 'This message was left for me on the course. Only someone who knows my habits would have been sure that I would receive it.'

'On the course?'

'Yes. I make it my habit to play a round on my own at first light whenever the weather permits. It enables me to meet our groundsman somewhere on the course and issue any necessary instructions. Playing so early also affords me the luxury of uninterrupted practice. Then I go into the clubhouse to deal with the morning post and any members' queries which may be waiting for me. The man who penned this message seems to be playing a bizarre game with me.'

'He left this on one of the teeing grounds for you?'

'Nothing as random as that – there might just have been other golfers about, even if it was not very likely, and this message was meant for me alone. We have a hut on the thirteenth where golfers may shelter from bad weather. We erected it two years ago; it is very useful when there is a sudden downpour. This sheet had been left on the seat in there, where he knew I should discover it.'

Holmes looked for a moment at our visitor, standing foursquare on the rug with his back to the cheerful fire, solid and powerful, in full health and the prime of life. With his large and ruddy face and his now corrected moustache, he seemed the epitome of the respectable outdoor man. He certainly did not look the over-imaginative sort of fellow who would be frightened without good cause. Holmes picked up the sheet of paper which looked so unremarkable as it lay upon our table and read aloud its sinister opening phrases:

BE WARNED BY WHAT HAS HAPPENED. IF YOU PERSIST IN YOUR DESIRE TO CARRY AWAY GOLF TROPHIES, YOU WILL NOT LONG SURVIVE IN THIS WORLD.

He glanced again at our visitor. 'This certainly seems to be aimed specifically at you, Mr Bullimore. Although it could in theory have been found by anyone in that shelter, the writer seems confident that your eyes would see it first. That argues someone very familiar with your daily routine. Do you know of anyone close to you who has shown any signs of personal hostility?'

No. I've thought about it, of course, but I haven't come up with anyone. It seems too fantastic.'

'Murder always does, Mr Bullimore. That is one of the things which murderers rely upon.'

I saw Bullimore give a little start at the mention of that awful word, and I may even have winced a little myself at the bluntness of it, for Holmes now said, with the irritation which often revealed itself when he was excited, 'Come, gentlemen, let us be clear about this! That is what our mysterious correspondent is threatening, if we are to take him seriously. Though "You will not long survive in this world" is a curiously convoluted way of putting it. Forgive me, Mr Bullimore, but I need to know about your domestic arrangements.'

Alfred Bullimore looked a little puzzled at this abrupt change of tack. Then his heavy features broke into a smile.

'I do not have a wife, Mr Homes. My passion, everyone tells me, is for golf, and it leaves me no room for intimate domestic bliss. I live comfortably enough, in a rented house near the course at Blackheath. I have a woman who comes in each morning to clean, but no other domestic staff. I find I eat at home too little to need a cook, and I prefer to be independent of a valet.' He glanced down at his russet tweeds and allowed himself a small amusement at his own expense. 'My dress, as you can see, is simple and varies little. My sisters have often taken me to task about it, but one does not have to humour sisters as one might a wife.'

Holmes nodded impatiently. 'What about the previous communications, the ones you have so unfortunately destroyed? Were they addressed to you by name?'

Bullimore frowned in concentration. 'No. I think the first ones were rather more general than this. I thought it was some lunatic who was threatening the club at large. As I say, I didn't take them very seriously, so I cannot remember much detail.'

'Lunatics must always be taken seriously, Mr Bullimore. They are dangerous people. We may have one here. Our task is to prevent him doing serious harm. You had better tell us what you can remember of these earlier warnings which have so regrettably disappeared.'

Bullimore was clearly stung by this reiteration of the importance of the earlier messages. 'Damn it all, sir, I didn't come here for a lecture! I threw away the earlier stuff because I thought it was drivel. I've never believed that anonymous writers should be afforded the dignity of a serious response.'

'An eminently worthy moral standpoint, Mr Bullimore.

But you are giving this one a serious response now, or you wouldn't have come hotfoot to Baker Street with his latest missive. And rightly so: I think the chap who wrote this is bent upon mischief. He doesn't appear to have many morals, and that is something we have to take into account, if we are to deal with him as he deserves. You had better tell us what you can remember of his earlier correspondence.'

Alfred Bullimore looked down at his large hands, watching them twining and untwining almost as if they belonged to someone else entirely as he spoke. 'I can see now that you're right, Sherlock Holmes; I should have kept these earlier notes. But you must remember that you have an experience of such things that I do not. Well, they were in envelopes, unlike this one, and they were hand-written, I think.'

'The more the pity that we do not have them, then. The science of calligraphy has advanced quickly in the last twenty years, so that writers give away much more of themselves than they realise. I have a monograph at present in preparation on the subject. Would you say it was a literate hand which penned those warnings?'

Bullimore worked his thick fingers furiously for a moment, then shrugged in frustration. 'I couldn't say, to be honest. It seemed a round and reasonably fluent hand, as far as I can remember it.'

'What about spelling and syntax?'

'Quite good, I think. I'm no schoolmaster, and you will understand that I was more concerned with the contents than the expression in these damned scrawls, but I'm sure I would have noticed any glaring transgressions of grammar.'

'Right. We assume someone who is literate, then.'

'Or someone who has got someone literate to write his messages out for him,' I said. It seemed quite some time since I had been able to contribute to this discussion, and I was glad to show my old friend that I was still alert.

Holmes smiled, as one might do when indulging a precocious child. 'Indeed, Watson. As always, you prevent us from flying too far from the known facts. The fruits of your medical training, I expect. Too much deduction from too small an observation is a dangerous thing. But this seems unlikely to be a case with much collusion involved. However, let us assume merely the obvious until we know a little more. Our man is someone with an intimate knowledge of the movements of Mr Bullimore. He is also both clever and lucky, two valuable attributes for a serious villain.'

Our visitor nodded, then looked puzzled. 'I can see that he knows a lot about me – must do, I suppose, from what's happened so far. I can't say it's a pleasant feeling to know one's being spied upon. But clever? And lucky?'

'Clever to have got thus far without your having the slightest idea who he might be. A man who watches the moments for his messages, and words them carefully. And lucky in that the one message of his which has been placed in the hands of his adversary is the only one which tells us nothing. Or very little.'

Holmes eyed the sheet upon the table for a second or two again, seemed about to pick it up, and then thought better of it. 'There are certain things suggested, nevertheless, by this sheet and the manner in which it has been delivered into our hands. But I prefer not to speculate upon anything so nebulous at present.'

Holmes turned to me with one of those magisterial

gestures with which he was wont to set the action in hand. 'I believe it is time for you to have a little winter exercise, Watson. You had better go out to Blackheath and have yourself a game of golf, I think.'

'But Holmes, I don't play the game. Well, not seriously, like Mr Bullimore here. It must be years since I last –'

'It will come back, Watson, surely? A simple enough pastime, like riding a velocipede, I'm sure. You didn't think I'd forgotten those golf sticks which lie neglected behind the wardrobe in our attic, did you? Why, I heard you up there retrieving them only the other day, when you thought I was immersed in your sensationalised account in *The Strand Magazine* of what you were pleased to call "The Affair of the Blue Carbuncle".'

'I was merely removing the dust of many months! And in any case I couldn't possibly –'

'You would deny yourself the innocent pleasure of a little gentle exercise, when Mr Bullimore's safety – nay, his very life may be at stake?'

Now who's being sensational, I thought. 'Surely there are other and more efficient methods of estimating just what degree of danger surrounds Mr Bullimore? I can't think there is any real reason for me to go making a fool of myself.'

'Modest as ever, Watson. One of your finest qualities. But even virtues can be taken to excess. And how else are we to find out about the people who surround Mr Bullimore without putting our quarry on his guard? An innocent venture upon the links by an enthusiastic and slightly over-weight medical man will scarcely excite comment around the club at Blackheath. The exercise may even be therapeutic for you, Watson. And I shall look forward to your report with lively interest.'

As usual when he was determined upon something, Holmes carried all before him, as inexorably as an incoming tide. Alfred Bullimore had looked scarcely more enthusiastic about the suggestion than I had – I imagine he did not relish the prospect of having to guide a hopeless novice round his course any more than I did being that novice – but there was logic after all in Holmes's argument. I would excite no more comment than any other enthusiastic but unskilled golfer, and I might be able to size up the situation without exciting suspicion. I had after all been trained by the best of all practitioners of such arts, Sherlock Holmes, however execrable my golf might be.

It was agreed within minutes that I should present myself at Blackheath Golf Club on the following day, and our guest left the house with a much greater appearance of equanimity than he had entered it.

I went up to the attic and retrieved the canvas bag of golf clubs from behind the old wardrobe. They were covered with dust, but I found a small bottle of linseed oil at the back of a drawer and rubbed the hickory of the shafts back to something near its original shade. Shutting the door carefully so that I should not be detected and mocked by my companion, I checked my posture with the brassie in front of the wardrobe's full-length mirror. It did not look too bad, but when I essayed a tentative swing, I nearly hit the big earthenware jug upon the wash-stand.

I put the club hastily away and descended to find our living-room obscured with clouds of blue-grey smoke and heavy with the oppressive scent of the Scottish mixture.

Holmes was puffing vigorously and contentedly on a Meerschaum. 'This case promises a certain interest, Watson. Already there are certain intriguing elements. We shall know more after your visit to Blackheath. And you have already been at work on the instruments of your enjoyment; such enthusiasm is highly commendable. But go easy on the linseed oil, and be careful when you experiment with that brassie: Mrs Hudson would not be pleased if you damaged her furnishings.'

I gulped, glancing automatically towards the door I was sure I had shut to preserve my privacy. No doubt you smelt the linseed oil about me, Holmes, though how on earth you can smell anything when you are at the centre of that odious emission from your pipe, I don't know. But how the dickens can you know that I have been checking my address position with a brassie?'

He smiled expansively; he would I'm sure have been disappointed if I had not asked him for an explanation. 'A simple enough deduction, surely, old friend? There is a small smear of linseed oil, obviously from the butt of a club, on your shirt just above your belt, at the spot where a less charitable man than me might detect a tendency to *embonpoint*. It is obviously too high to have been made by one of the shorter iron clubs. The length indicates a driver or a brassie. I merely assumed that your natural modesty would lead you to try the easier of those two clubs first after a period away from the game.'

I sighed. 'I fear I shall make a fool of myself with Alfred Bullimore. You put me in some embarrassing situations at times, Holmes.'

'Nonsense. You will cope, Watson, as always.' Holmes

waved away my objections with all the arrogance of one who had never attempted this most complex of all games. 'And we shall be able to assess the true dangers of the situation at Blackheath. Remember that that is the real purpose of your excursion. I shall meditate for a little while longer on the contradictions which have already presented themselves to me in this case. But do not be alarmed. It does not seem to me more than a one-pipe problem, at present.' He lay back complacently in his chair and puffed smoke energetically at the high ceiling of the room, happy to be confronting a challenge to his powers once again.

At least there was no more violin-playing in the hours which followed.

TWO

The next morning dawned even brighter than that fatal Tuesday when Bullimore had come to us with his bizarre tale of mischief on the links.

I had half-hoped for a renewal of the winter rains, so that I might excuse myself from the exposure of my golfing skills which Holmes had so gleefully arranged for me. Instead, the sun rose clear and golden above city gardens whitened by a slight frost. As I collected the last of my clubs and looked out from the attic window, I could see far across the city. For the first time in months, I could see how the work was progressing on the lofty nave of the new Roman Catholic cathedral in Westminster. The red-brick elevations were clearly visible, rising proud and impressive above the urban haze, though work had not yet begun on the slender campanile, which we were told would rival that in Venice's St Mark's Square.

There was little time to dwell on such delights, for Holmes dispatched me south to Blackheath after a hurried breakfast. His haste was almost unseemly; he had a hansom waiting outside the door of 221B when I came down the stairs a little self-consciously, with my bag of golf sticks slung over the left shoulder of my tweed jacket. The great man could be almost a schoolboy in his impatience once he felt that the game was afoot. Or perhaps when it was merely stirring, in this case: after a good night's sleep, my own feeling was that there could scarcely be very much in this affair, that Bullimore had exaggerated any danger there might be. I confess this readily; it was not the first time I was wrong, nor the last.

It was quite a distance to Blackheath, but I enjoyed the morning and the ride, thrusting aside the apprehension I felt at the sporting ordeal which awaited me at the end of my journey.

The Thames was busy with barges as we crossed it and moved out through Greenwich; gilded by the low sun from the east, the river had a picturesque and busy aspect which might have excited Canaletto in the pale, clear light of that morning of very early spring.

I got the cabby to drop me outside the gates of the golf club at Blackheath. Golf then was still played on the ancient heath itself, and a notice in the quaint clubhouse proclaimed that this was the oldest club in England. Fortunately for me and my rusty skills, golf then was not the popular game it has become in the thirty years since. Nowadays people like Mr Walter Hagen have crossed the Atlantic to win our championships, making a living from simply playing the game, and increasing its popularity with the public in the process. But on that Wednesday morning, Blackheath Golf Club (it did not then have the 'Royal' epithet in its title) was a quiet place.

Alfred Bullimore must have been looking out for me, for he came out through the heavy oak door of the Secretary's office as I entered the building. 'Good morning, Dr Watson, and welcome to our humble premises,' he said affably. He beamed beneath what was this time a perfectly waxed moustache, and was clearly more at ease in this familiar environment than he had been in our rooms at Baker Street. He took me on a tour of the building, whispering to me that it was no more than he would have done for any visitor.

It reminded me that I was here to observe the situation and those involved in it, while playing the part of a normal golfer. I took a keen interest not only in the design of the building but in the people we met as we walked through it, for I knew that Sherlock Holmes was the most exacting of taskmasters when it came to the report I should have to deliver to him at the end of the day.

I paid particular attention to the employees, for these were people who were permanently about the place, who might be expected to know the daily movements of the Secretary who controlled their lives. We had already agreed that the mysterious threats and the villainies which had already occurred must have been perpetrated by someone who had both an intimate knowledge of Bullimore's habits and some reason, real or imagined, to hate him.

There was a chef in the kitchens, a powerful man who could easily have perpetrated the attack on Captain Osborne and his dog in the darkness. He spoke quite good English, with a pronounced French accent. I noted his massive forearms, but he seemed on good enough terms with the man who employed him, though to my mind he did not afford him the due deference; Alfred Bullimore was after all a gentleman, strictly an Honorary Secretary of the club, and I thought this Marcel Lebrun should have been rather more conscious of the fact. Perhaps it was his Gallic temperament – I am told there is less consciousness of rank in France, but I have never explored this – or perhaps he was merely a very good cook and relied on his popularity with the members to allow him such liberties. However, I was not able to explore his feelings towards Bullimore in any detail, as this would surely have aroused suspicion.

I had the same difficulty with another employee of the club. When we went back into the Secretary's office, I was surprised to find a pretty woman of about thirty sitting demurely at the large Remington typewriter. 'Mrs Ross comes in to help with our paperwork on three mornings a week,' said Bullimore expansively. 'Just for two hours on each occasion, but there seem to be double the number of letters we had even three years ago, when I took up the reins as secretary. And Christobel – she will forgive me the informality, I know – is most efficient, as well as being an ornament in the club which our regular members much appreciate.'

Mrs Ross blushed most prettily at the compliment, which I thought inappropriate. I was surprised to hear him introduce the lady's first name into the conversation at this first meeting. She was a winsome creature, and I wondered as we moved out of the room whether Alfred Bullimore was as proof against the attractions of the fair sex as he had claimed on his visit to 221B on the previous day. If he had trifled with the affections of the lady, she could well cause trouble. Frustrated passion is one of the strongest drives towards violence, as Dr Freud was to demonstrate to the more conservative members of my profession in the years which followed.

At my request, Bullimore left me for a few minutes with

the three members who sat in front of a merrily crackling fire in the drawing-room of the club. If they were here at this time of the day, they were clearly men who spent a lot of time at the club, and thus candidates for the role of perpetrator of the curious and escalating violence which was besetting it. The oldest of them turned out to be the very Captain Osborne who had been the victim of the assault on the course, but he was able to add nothing to what I already knew of the incident. He seemed most upset by the damage to his small dog, which had had to be put down after the incident. He assured me that his own injuries were mending fast, that all he wanted now was 'five minutes alone with that scoundrel with my walking stick when he's caught'.

I seized upon this opening to discuss the possibilities of the unmasking of the culprit with the others, but they were not very communicative. The larger of them, who had been introduced to me as Herbert Robinson, seemed to be in trade in the city. He clearly thought it a pity that I had been told anything at all of these unfortunate events at the club. 'Best kept within the family, these things, if you ask me. Next thing you know, we'll have the peelers in, stamping all over the place and finding nothing.' He rose and stood with his back to the fire, looked over my head, and blew out a long sigh of resentment.

I was tempted to tell him that no less a man than Sherlock Holmes had been retained, which meant that something certainly would be found, but I bit my lip and stared into the fire. I knew I must keep the cover of being merely a chance visitor in search of a game of golf if I was not to alert the quarry to the fact that he was being pursued. As if he caught that very thought, the heavy man in front of me glared suddenly down into my face and said, 'Friend of Bullimore's, are you?'

I said that I was, that I was a medical man back from a spell in India who was hoping to rediscover a passion for the game he had not been able to play for several years. It was the story Bullimore and I had agreed, and as you see it had elements of truth in it: Holmes had taught me long ago what all criminals know, that the best lies are those which stick as closely as possible to the truth. Both of my listeners seemed to accept my *bona fides* as soon as they discovered that I was a medical practitioner. It is a pleasing effect which I have often noticed. Of course, you must remember that this was in 1896, before Dr Crippen and others had brought such unwelcome publicity to our profession!

The third club member before that cheerful fire was more relaxed. He had his own firm of solicitors, who acted for the club whenever necessary, and was looking forward to arranging the prosecution of our villain in due course. He quizzed me a little about my friendship with Bullimore, and I divined through his caution that he had no great love for the Secretary. I hastened to assure him that mine was quite a shallow and recent acquaintance, hoping to draw him on into some revelations about the source and depth of his antipathy to Bullimore. But he played a bat as straight and solid as W.G. Grace's to my probings, and I did not get very far before Bullimore himself returned to collect me.

'Not a very forthcoming chap, that,' I said to Alfred as we went into the hall outside.

'Edward Frobisher? Oh, he's all right, I suppose. I try to tread a bit carefully with him, because of what happened three years ago. He was rather expecting to become Secretary of the club when I did, you see. He'd been a member for years longer than I had, and his firm had acted for the club over legal agreements about playing on the old common land. But the members seemed to think I was a better bet, even though I'd been around only for a few years. There was no money involved, of course: it's strictly an honorary post. I was a much better golfer than Edward, and that certainly counted for quite a lot.'

He said it modestly enough, but his pride in his prowess came out in the satisfied silence which followed it. I was left wondering whether resentment which began with a mere blow to one's *amour propre* could grow into a violent, even perhaps murderous, hatred. It didn't seem likely – but then it was obvious to me by now that the solution to this strange problem was never going to be a logical one. Common-sense rarely drives a man to murder. Or a woman: I glimpsed the demure but comely figure of Mrs Christobel Ross again as I passed the window of the Secretary's office with my clubs.

I was on my way to the caddiemaster's shed. Alfred Bullimore, as he had told us yesterday, always carried his clubs, but he had tactfully suggested that I should seek the aid of a caddie to carry mine. I did not like the glance he had given to my waistline as he said this, but it was no doubt well-meant advice. And I had other things in mind. From what I had heard of their drinking habits and their irregular lifestyles, caddies were an unruly lot. Men who slept under hedges and were dependent on irregular payments, everyone said; such fellows were always likely to turn desperate. Of the men who were habitually around the club, they were in my book the likeliest candidates for serious villainy.

But it seemed I was doomed to frustration as far as this avenue was concerned. The caddiemaster's shed was locked and deserted. But an enquiry from a passing groundsman elicited the information that the caddiemaster doubled as a club-repairer and might be found within the professional's shop. I found him there sure enough, putting a new hickory shaft into a battered-looking cleek. When I asked about a caddie, he shook his head apologetically. 'There isn't too much call for them, mid-week, sir. We have half a dozen regular, reliable men on Saturdays and Sundays, but most of them have other work during the week, you see. There'll be a couple of men around this afternoon, but they're already booked by two of our members, I'm afraid. There was one chap around about half an hour ago who was looking for a bag to carry, but he's not one of our regulars, so I couldn't say how good he'd be on the course.'

'Better than the man he'd be carrying for, I wouldn't mind wagering!' I laughed ruefully.

There was no sign of the fellow when I looked around the outbuildings, so I threw my own bag reluctantly across my shoulder and made for the first tee. But I was still thirty yards short of it when a dishevelled figure emerged from the bushes, touched his frayed cap, and offered to carry my clubs. His black hobnailed boots had seen much better days, he was muffled to the eyebrows in an assortment of ragged woollens, and I did not much like the look of him. But I was by this time feeling thoroughly unnerved by the imminent prospect of exposing my game to Alfred Bullimore, whom the members in the clubhouse had assured me was a

Titan in this exacting sport. Any help seemed to me better than none; the tatterdemalion figure was duly engaged, for the princely sum of one shilling and sixpence, which he assured me in a thick Scottish accent was the going rate.

'I'll just watch ye for a hole or two, sir, before offering any advice. Get the feel of your game, ye see.' He handed me my aged driver, teed my yellowing ball on a handful of sand, and stood magisterially over my canvas bag as I prepared for my first stroke in several years.

To give the fellow his due, he certainly earned his money on that bright morning. Whilst Alfred Bullimore hit every fairway and almost every green with monotonous regularity, I proceeded to find every kind of trouble on that blasted heath. Sand, bushes, heather, even the few patches of winter water; my ball sought them out as if it were a hound on the scent of trouble. Bullimore gave me a shot a hole, and handled the match with masterful ease.

I could not blame my misfortunes on my caddie. He had an eagle eye, and moved forward after each stroke to discover my ball with unerring accuracy. After two holes, he had sized up my game, and generally handed me the right club as I approached my ball. When I insisted upon hitting a spoon from a difficult lie in a desperate attempt at recovery, he sighed heavily as he handed it to me. He was waiting for me when I arrived panting with frustration at the result of this effort; this time he had my niblick out of the bag and handed it to me with the injunction, 'Just swing easy now, sir, and keep yer heed still.'

I glared at him but tried to do as I was told, and the ball sketched an appealing parabola against the blue sky and almost reached the green. I began to ask his advice on the greens before I putted. After surveying the line from several viewpoints on the first occasion, my man gave me the advice that 'It might just be slightly straight, sir.' I looked at him suspiciously, but there was no sign of humour on the little I could see of his Caledonian countenance, swaddled as it was against the cold by cap and muffler. The putt proved indeed to be perfectly straight.

I improved a little in the second half of the round when I took my caddie's advice, which was generally to be less ambitious. But the match was beyond retrieval, and over the last few holes I could not but admire the majesty of my opponent's play. Alfred Bullimore was indeed a splendid golfer, with an ability far beyond anything my limited experience of this frustrating game had previously accorded me. He was, moreover, totally concentrated upon his own game. When I apologised for the third time for not providing him with a decent match, he waved the thought away airily. He was, he explained, used to winning easily; his only concern nowadays was with the excellence of his own golf and with bringing consistency to it. He had beaten the bogey of the course (what I believe is now beginning to be called the par) by two strokes on that bright, crisp morning, and that had meant the match was entirely satisfactory for him, however erratic the opposition might have been.

I began to perceive how such a man might be unpopular.

I gave my caddie a tip of sixpence on top of the fee we had agreed, for he had proved more helpful and long-suffering than I had ever anticipated. When he had my silver florin safely in his hand, he ventured the opinion that I 'could become a gey wee golfer, with a wee bit o' practice, and the right man on the bag.'

I preferred to cut short any discussion on my prowess, but I remembered for the first time in two hours the real purpose of my visit to Blackheath. The ragged fellow was obviously anxious to be away with his booty, but I prevailed upon him to say what he knew of the feelings of the other caddies at the club.

He was not a regular, he said, so he could not speak in any detail. But he hinted in his thick Glaswegian tones that any man who played as much as Mr Bullimore did without ever using a caddie was not providing employment among the fraternity, and thus could scarcely expect much popularity with them. When I pressed him, he said a little reluctantly that he thought the Secretary, though undoubtedly a fine golfer, 'a mite conceited' about his prowess and with 'no thought for the lives of poorer folk about the place'. This he thought, was the view of most of the caddies, though whether any of them had more personal cause for resentment he could not say. Or was not willing to say, I thought darkly. But I let him go with that. I could scarcely expect him to jeopardise his future chances of employment by saying anything more definite against the Secretary. And my own cover was in danger: I was uncomfortably aware that the Scotsman was eyeing me with some suspicion above his muffler. He disappeared into the bushes whence he had come, with the same swift, stooping gait with which he had arrived.

The clubhouse was a livelier place at lunchtime than it had been at ten o'clock. The members were willing enough to talk, but I excused myself on the grounds of fatigue and retired to the other end of the members' room with my copy of *The Times* and a stiff whisky. I listened to the rising tide of conversation at the other end of the room, picking up what I could of the members' opinions of their Secretary. My impression was of a man more respected than loved. He was clearly efficient enough in his secretarial duties, though some people thought the employment of Mrs Ross an extravagance not warranted by the work involved. There were a couple of male sniggers about the relationship which might exist between Bullimore and his attractive assistant, but I fear such remarks are to be expected in all-male communities like this. Bullimore's golf was a much admired source of wonderment among his golfing peers. But I caught adverse comments upon his single-mindedness and his lack of humour.

When Alfred Bullimore himself emerged by prior arrangement and took me into the dining-room for a late lunch, one or two people looked at us curiously, but I carefully gave no sign that I had overheard any of their conversation. We were the only two people eating at this hour, and the Secretary asked me cautiously if I had discovered anything of interest. I said that I had picked up a few things, but wouldn't wish to comment until I had reported back to Sherlock Holmes, who was after all the professional in these matters.

He nodded. 'I wonder he did not come here himself,' he said. 'I do not wish to denigrate your efforts, Dr Watson, and I am sure you have gathered all that could really be expected from such a visit, but I would have expected Holmes to attend here himself, rather than sending an assistant.'

'Mr Holmes could hardly have done that without exciting comment and putting your unknown opponent upon his guard,' I pointed out stiffly. 'He suggested that I might make a preliminary visit because I could do so without suspicion in the guise of a golfer. My friend has never played the game, whereas I have some experience of it, though you might not have thought so today.'

'You might perhaps become a fair player, with practice,' he said with a shade of condescension. 'But it seems that, as a detective, you have your limitations.'

Surely the man did not need to be quite so blunt! I said coldly, 'This was merely a preliminary visit, a reconnoitring mission. I have gathered from it all that might reasonably be expected. There are certain things of interest which have emerged. I shall report them to my colleague when I return to Baker Street.'

At this point the chef, Marcel Lebrun, emerged to ask if we were happy with the food, which was excellent. It was an unnecessary intrusion, I thought, reinforcing the tendency to indecorum I had already noted in the man. I changed the subject in his presence, for I had already marked the Frenchman down as one of the men with ample opportunity to have perpetrated the messages and the damage to people and property which had already occurred.

Despite his questions, Alfred Bullimore did not seem much disappointed that no definite pointers had emerged from my visit. He appeared nowhere near as perturbed as when he had burst into our rooms at Baker Street. But he had had time to compose himself since then. And in his own domain, where he was a dominating figure both on and off the golf course, he clearly felt much more confident.

Wrapped in a rug in the back of the hansom, fortified by

my excellent lunch and half a bottle of claret, I dozed my way home to the soft rhythm of the horse's hooves ahead of me. It had not been entirely a wasted day; in that mellow twilight, I thought that perhaps I would take up this challenging sport of golf, to provide exercise and a challenge in my middle age.

As for the main purpose of my visit to Blackheath, I felt that the affair of the frightened golfer would prove after all to be a matter of minor excitement.

THREE

I was naturally eager to discuss my day with Holmes, but he called from his room that he was about to have a bath, Mrs Hudson having assured him that there was enough hot water to do so. After his eagerness to send me on my mission in the morning, I had anticipated he would be impatient for news, but apparently the earlier urgency had deserted him. I was always worried by violent mood changes in him since the serious illness he had endured in the middle 'nineties, but there was nothing for it but to wait until after dinner to discuss things, as he suggested. At least there was no sign that he had been using the cocaine of which I disapproved so heartily.

Normally he was not much interested in food, but on that Wednesday evening he savoured Mrs Hudson's mutton pie with such relish that I suspected he was deliberately delaying me. Even when our landlady had cleared the table, he insisted upon fitting a new mantle to the gas light in the middle of the room, a domestic improvement I had never seen him effect before. It was not until we were sitting with a glass of port and he had gone through the ritual of selecting and lighting one of the largest of his cherrywood pipes that he said, 'Come then, Watson, fire away with your findings.'

I studied the glowing end of my cigar for a moment, being determined by now to be as leisurely about this as my old companion. 'I have nothing sensational to report. But when you determined that I should arrive at Blackheath as a casual golfer, you set certain restrictions upon me. I think I have discovered as much as could reasonably be expected on a preliminary visit of this sort.'

'Come, Watson, you are too cautious. You adopt the phrases of your profession. The case, like the patient, is as well as "could reasonably be expected". You can do better than that. No doubt after your experiences with me you observed things at Blackheath more carefully than you used to do. Let us now hear what you deduced from what you saw.' He stretched his legs to put his feet upon the fender and puffed clouds of grey smoke over the mantelpiece and its ornaments.

'Very well, Holmes. But there are limits to what can be achieved on a mission such as the one I undertook today, and you must surely realise that.'

'Of course. You were to provide the groundwork on which we build, not the finished building. You have provided me with the foundations in the past, Watson, as in that affair on Dartmoor with the Baskervilles, which you tell me you plan to write up in due course, and you will no doubt do so again in the future. Indeed, you may already have performed a similar task in this small but intriguing problem. So proceed, please, without further diffidence.'

'Well, the Blackheath club and the course are more or less as I expected them to be. The clubhouse is a comfortable place, with good facilities and a number of permanent staff, all of whom are obviously familiar with the workings of the place and the movements of our friend Mr Bullimore. The course is pleasant but exacting – rather too much so, I fear, for the present state of my golf.' Holmes smiled here in a manner that I thought unnecessarily patronising, but I ignored him and produced my notes. 'When it comes to locating our culprit, there seem to be four possible areas: the paid staff within the club; the membership; those outdoor staff who work on the course; and the miscellaneous group of men who act as caddies to the members.'

'Come, Watson, "more matter, with less art" please. You are in your Polonius vein, and you must remember what happened to that old bore.'

I was nettled by this, but I have to admit that I had been sounding a little pompous, even to my own ears. It was his own fault for making me wait so long to report. 'Very well. I have already identified two members of the club staff as being of interest. The first is Marcel Lebrun, the chef.'

'A Frenchman, by the sound of him, and therefore clearly suspect in John Watson's book.' Holmes lay even further back in his armchair, puffed smoke at the ceiling and smiled after it.

'Really, Holmes! I noted merely that Lebrun would certainly have been around the club at the time of the incidents with the broken golf sticks, that he knows probably better than anyone the daily movements of Alfred Bullimore; that he is a powerful man, who would have certainly have been capable of inflicting the physical damage on old Captain Osborne and his unfortunate dog.'

'Opportunity then. And motive?'

'Nothing very tangible yet, I have to admit. All I can say is that I noted his attitude when he came into the dining-room at the end of our lunch. I considered him less deferential to Mr Bullimore than I should have expected him to be.'

'And therefore a murderer? Yes, I see. Well, this radical attitude to an employer, when combined with a Gallic background, makes out a pretty damning case against the blackguard. Do we really need to look any further?'

'Really, Holmes, if you cannot be serious, I shall keep my thoughts to myself!' I glared at him, but he refused to look back at me, continuing to study the rose in the centre of the ceiling above the newly renovated gas light. 'There are other possibilities, of course. This is nothing other than the preliminary survey of the facts which you asked me to undertake. There is, for example, a woman who works closely with the Secretary. A young and attractive woman.'

'Aaah! Excellent, Watson. A woman always brings variety and interest to a list of suspects, I find. And a young and attractive one doubly so. Perhaps she has already touched the heart of the chivalrous Dr Watson.'

'Really, Holmes, if you cannot be serious, I shall –'

'And if the fair lady can affect the judgement of even so cool and objective a judge as John Watson, how much more turbulence may she have brought to the breasts of younger and more impulsive men! Speak on swiftly, pray, before my excitement overcomes me!'

I began to wonder what my companion had been up to during the day whilst I was conducting my assiduous research at Blackheath. Perhaps the syringe had after all been out of its drawer again, as the user took advantage of my absence. Or perhaps I had merely caught him in one of his tiresomely playful moods, of the kind he indulged in when he was withholding some piece of information from me: yet on this occasion it was obvious that I must know more than he. I said heavily, 'The lady's name is Mrs Christobel Ross. For your information, I have scarcely spoken to her. She is a young widow. As far as I could observe, she is a pretty but demure lady. I have to report that there was some speculation among the members about her relationship with Alfred Bullimore, but no more than I should have expected from an all-male gathering with the whisky in free circulation. Men with time on their hands often speculate on these lines. There is probably nothing more than a few ungentlemanly sniggers behind it.'

'Let us hope so, Watson. But in a case which has obviously baffled my worthy assistant, any area such as this must be explored.'

'So I thought, Holmes. There is probably nothing in it, as I say, but if there is, well . . . "Hell hath no fury like a woman scorned" and all that.'

'"And all that", as you say, Watson. The quotation is not quite exact, but it will serve us well enough. The lady merits further investigation. Are there any other such areas?'

'Well, there is the membership, of course. All gentlemen, the ones I saw. Of course, there will be many more of them around at the weekend. But I don't think Blackheath is the kind of place to encourage people other than gentlemen to take up the game. And the game itself, of course . . . '

'Does not encourage people without a certain standing and affluence to participate. Quite. Unless, of course, they are very good; in which case they become professionals, and show everyone how the game should be played.'

I looked at him suspiciously. 'Alfred Bullimore is not a

professional. And he plays the game of golf very well indeed.'

'Hmm. Well enough, perhaps, to have excited a certain envy among his fellow members at Blackheath?'

'I did notice a degree of resentment, yes. Not without cause. I found him a fine player, but insufferably self-centred and self-satisfied about his own game. Almost obsessed, I should say. I was taught to keep games in perspective.'

'And so you have, my old friend. But no doubt you gave the bounder a run for his money today, with your flair for the sport restored?'

I did not care to report the details of my trouncing to Holmes in this mood. 'I did not play very well, I think. But that is not relevant to my report.'

'Sadly, that is the case. I should have enjoyed a detailed account of your round. But no doubt your natural modesty forbids it. However, you say the members are not over-fond of their Secretary. Did you notice any of them with a particular feeling against him?'

'Nothing that stood out as a real pointer to our culprit. But I noted a couple of names.' I turned back to my notes. 'The first was Herbert Robinson. He thought the matter should have been kept within the club – thought it a bit off that a casual visitor to the club like me should even know about it.'

'A common enough view, if perhaps mistaken in this case. The gentry in Britain are always happy to hush up a scandal, until it becomes serious enough to alarm them. Then they are only too happy to call for our assistance. Robinson didn't suspect you of being anything more than a visiting golfer, though?'

'No, I don't think so. I took care not to press him too hard for information. He worried about the police stirring up a hornet's nest without finding anything useful. He went on about "having the peelers tramping all over the place".'

Holmes smiled. 'We have seen some instances of police heavy-handedness in our time, have we not, Watson? Though I should not care to say so in the hearing of our friends Lestrade and Gregson. Well-meaning chaps, those inspectors, but we've seen them flounder a little.'

I smiled in turn. Holmes had saved red faces at Scotland Yard often enough to be permitted his little satisfaction. 'Herbert Robinson had no very high opinion of our police force, anyway. I suspect most of the members would agree with them about keeping their troubles within the club, so long as it was a matter of petty pilfering or minor damage to property. But they have now had quite a nasty attack on an ailing member – I saw Captain Osborne while I was at Blackheath – with his dog hit so hard it had to be put down and the gentleman himself lucky not to suffer worse damage in the dark. Robinson opposed any outside investigation in old Osborne's presence: it seemed to me a bit insensitive, so I noted his attitude.'

'Quite rightly. But you mentioned a second member who excited your attention.'

'Yes. For more tangible reasons, I think. Edward Frobisher is the name. A lawyer, though I think affluent enough to let his practice run itself most of the time. He spends a lot of time at the club, and he was expecting that the members would make him Secretary when they gave the job to Bullimore three years ago. Alfred was a much more recent member, though patently the best golfer in the club. It's only an honorary post, so there was no material loss involved, but Frobisher's pride was obviously hurt. I don't know how deep his bitterness runs, but he clearly dislikes Bullimore. I have to say that from the casual conversations I overheard around the bar at lunch time, the Secretary did not seem to be a particularly popular chap. For instance, there was some amusement over the damage to his bag of clubs that he told us about – people only began to treat our villain seriously when he attacked poor old Osborne. But I mention Frobisher as he seems to be one with a specific reason to hate our client.'

Holmes had set aside his pipe; his attention was thoroughly upon me now. 'And what is your informed opinion, Watson? Did you have a feeling after your visit to Blackheath that our offender is likely to come from within the membership of the club?'

I had puzzled a little about this on the way home before I had dozed off in the cab. 'I don't think so. The members are well-educated gentlemen. I can't see any of them getting up to the kind of mischief and violence we have heard about from Bullimore.'

Holmes smiled. 'You have enough experience by now to know that no section of society is exempt from evil, Watson. You have helped me to bring to justice quite a few heinous criminals who masqueraded as gentlemen. You have chronicled many of these happenings, bringing their crimes to a wider audience. You really must get rid of your prejudices. They are a great hindrance to an open mind, and it is the open mind which responds best to the clues we shall unearth.'

'Perhaps so. But you asked me merely about where our culprit was *likeliest* to come from, and I gave my opinion. I am sure there are more desperate fellows around the place than the members: I think you are more likely to find your villain among them, that is all.'

'You are a sturdy defender of your class, Watson. I suppose that is no very bad thing, despite the evidence that has accrued against that stance in the course of our previous investigations. Where, then, do you think we shall find our man?'

'Well, I didn't get any chance at all to see the men who work on the course. There are two men fully employed, I believe, and one more occasional labourer. They obviously know the course itself and the outbuildings of the club quite intimately, though Bullimore appears to think they are trustworthy.'

'And no doubt those poor fellows would be the immediate suspects when these happenings occurred around the club and on the course merely because of their humble station in life. So far, no one has been able to prove anything against them, though they have no doubt tried.'

I had not thought of that, but it was probably true. I said uncomfortably, 'There is one other sort of employee at the club, which is in my view most likely to provide our offender. I do not say that it is necessarily so, only that these men are in my view the most likely source of serious trouble.'

'I see. Tell us then of this den of thieves which awaits investigation.'

'I speak of the caddies at the club. They are not permanent employees, but men who come and go. No one, not even the caddiemaster, knows where most of them live. I suspect many of them have what the courts call no fixed abode. The best of them are the respectable unemployed. The worst of them are I fear little better than vagrants. You do not know much about golf, Holmes, but I have to tell you that the caddies have a terrible reputation for drunkenness and fighting among themselves.'

'I see. And were you able to sample the quality of the caddies at Blackheath?'

I shook my head in genuine regret. It was in this area that I had thought to have my best chance of discovering our villain; to have done so without the aid of Holmes would, I confess, have given me much pleasure. 'No. There being not much demand for their services on a weekday morning, they were not in attendance. I was lucky, indeed, to acquire the services of one of the breed, just when I thought I would have to carry my own clubs. A pretty desperate-looking fellow he was too. I have to admit he served his turn well enough on the course, but he looked as though he had spent the night under a hedgerow, and he departed swiftly with my payment for his services. I fear much of it has passed across the counter of some lowly inn by now.'

'But you say he was adequate on the course?'

'Competent enough, yes. A strange, wild fellow, with a stooping half-run once he had the clubs across his back. But I fancy he knew the game; he had a thick Scottish accent – they play the game a lot more up there, you know.'

'Indeed I do, Watson. I believe the Open Championship is to be played up there this year. At Muirfield.'

His knowledge was a constant source of wonderment to

me. As far as I knew, he had taken no interest in the game at all until Alfred Bullimore had arrived so precipitately on the previous morning. 'You know more than I do, I confess, Holmes. And I can claim a certain degree of proficiency in this game.'

'But not a great one, I believe.'

I was a little nettled by this, coming from one who as far as I knew had never even ventured upon a golf course. 'I am not as proficient as Mr Bullimore, certainly. Not by a long chalk. I grant you that. But I hit one or two shots in my round today of which I was quite proud. I am sure this ragged fellow who carried my clubs knew something of the game, and I think he was quite impressed on occasions. I believe he said something to that effect at the end of the round, though I cannot recall his words, nor imitate his Caledonian accent.'

'Ye could become a gey wee golfer with a wee bit o' practice, and the right man on your bag.' My companion looked steadily at the ceiling, nodding slowly.

'His very words, I believe! And in the same broad Scottish accent. But how on earth –'

'Glaswegian is easy enough, with a little practice. I dare say it would not deceive a native, but my efforts are good enough for the average Sassenach. Of which I suspect you are a splendid example, my old friend.'

'You mean that rascally fellow was you? But the clothes? The complexion?'

'Easy enough. I have plenty of rags in Mrs Hudson's cellar, as you should know, and a little theatrical grease-paint, mixed in this case with a little London grit, darkens the countenance quite alarmingly. I fancy you saw little enough of my face anyway, between that capacious muffler and my big cap. You should remember if you ever embark upon such deceptions that it is easy to over-elaborate: I flatter myself that the small scar I gave myself over the left eyebrow was not unduly lurid. It was certainly very convincing; I was so taken with it that I removed it only five minutes before your arrival back in the house. Mrs Hudson's maid was for a moment reluctant to let me in.'

'But – but the fellow who carried my clubs was an altogether shorter man. Really, Holmes, I can accept that you used someone who has reported back to you, but you must not try to convince me that you were that petty rogue.'

Having been recumbent for so long, Holmes suddenly sprang like a cat to his feet, moving swiftly to the other end of our living-room and back again in the very same swift, shambling gait as he had lately used on the golf course at Blackheath – for his movements now forced me to accept that it was he who had been my companion in the afternoon's sporting ordeal. 'I have told you before, Watson: the hardest thing of all in assuming a disguise is to take a foot off your natural height. You should recall that, for you recorded it in your notes for what I see you plan to call *The Adventure of the Empty House.*'

'When you pretended to be an elderly bookseller.'

'A much more difficult assumption than today's little task. I decided half a foot off my height would be enough today. But I was pleased with the walk I developed. I think you will agree I contrived to keep it consistent. And I did a good enough job on the course to warrant my fee, I say.' With a broad smile, he produced my silver florin from his trouser pocket and held it up triumphantly. It gleamed at me mockingly beneath the bright new gas-mantle.

I was forced to admit the disguise and my total deception by it. 'But you dispatched me from our door in a hansom. How on earth did you arrive at Blackheath before me? At least half an hour before me, if I am to believe the caddiemaster's report.'

'By taking a train, Watson: there is a simple explanation for most things. I consulted this month's *Bradshaw's* timetable last night and knew I could be there before you if I timed it right. Hence my anxiety to see you safely installed in your hansom this morning: had you delayed for two minutes longer, I should have missed my train.'

'But why, Holmes? If you merely wished to practise your wiles upon me, it was an elaborate and expensive enterprise. And one, I must say, in dubious taste. If you wish to take advantage of an old friend in such a way, then –'

'It was necessary, Watson. If you gave the matter a moment's thought, you would descend from your high horse. The caddies, as you say, are notoriously a fairly desperate crew, and therefore must be investigated. As you also found, there was no possible way for you to do that in your guise of a visiting golfer. A classic case for a little elementary disguise on my part.'

'And did you discover anything?'

'A little. Enough, perhaps, for our purposes at this stage. I found out who the regular caddies are and which ones live adjacent to the course. Two of them have convictions for violence and a third for petty larceny. I found nothing to connect any of them as yet with the dubious happening at Blackheath Golf Club, but I was able to make only the most superficial investigation in the time available.'

It made what I had thought my carefully weighed conclusions on the people I had listed seem like the vaguest ramblings. But I knew better than to disparage my friend's researches. 'How on earth did you find so much in so little time?'

He smiled. 'One of the gentlemen in question owed me a favour; I proved his innocence when the police accused him of a much more serious crime in '93. The police are a little over-eager in Blackheath still; you may recall that that is where the infamous Charles Peace fired upon a policeman and was arrested. My friend Goggins caddies a little himself, when he can get the work. He was willing enough to tell me what he could about his companions.'

Holmes's easy acquaintance with all classes of men had served us well before. Something else now struck me. 'But you displayed a knowledge of golf when you were carrying my clubs. You were even able to offer me useful advice, though you said yesterday you had no knowledge of the game.'

He regarded me steadily for a moment, his eyes crinkling a little with mirth. 'Nor have I, Watson. No knowledge worth having. But what I saw today confirmed my view that golf is in essence a simple enough game, which is made complicated by those who practise it. I studied your efforts in silence for three holes, then offered the advice which any dispassionate observer might have provided. In relation to your skills at the game, you were being quite absurdly over-ambitious. I merely attempted to make you work within your own limitations. You did not always listen to me, but when you did, you achieved some limited success, as much as you were capable of, from my assessment of your skills.'

I knew I was being teased, but I could not prevent myself rising to the bait. I felt my face reddening as I said, 'Let me tell you, Holmes, that the game is nothing like so simple as you imagine. If you would care to put your own skills to the test −'

'Watson, I should not be so foolish. Golf is not a pastime worthy of my attention. The analysis of what is required affords a certain simple satisfaction, but I have neither the time nor the inclination to acquire the physical skills involved. The study of crime shall remain my hobby as well as my life's work.'

I was more put out than I cared to admit by his comments on my golf. I rumbled on for a little about healthy minds needing the temples of healthy bodies, but I had heard him dismiss that argument too often before to have any hope of success. When he reverted to the subject of how I might best improve my golf, I said brusquely, 'Holmes, it has been a long day and I feel the need of my bed. Let us summarise matters, then leave things for the present. First, it now seems certain that the focus of our unknown villain's attentions is Alfred Bullimore himself. I have found a couple of members, Herbert Robinson and Edward Frobisher, who seem to have some reason for resentment against their Secretary. There may well be others. There is also a lady, Mrs Christobel Ross, who seems worthy of further investigation − Holmes, do take that supercilious smile off your face. There is in addition a French chef, Marcel Lebrun, who it seems to me may well entertain some grudge against Bullimore. For your part, you have thrown up several suspects among that dubious group of casual employees who act as caddies – the area I still think likeliest to provide our answer.'

'An estimable summary, Watson. Whenever you act as book-keeper and merely record the facts, I find your work admirable. It is only when you work our cases up into stories and are tempted towards the lurid and the dramatic that I find your style questionable. Now, even if we ignore as irrelevant the pleasures which were afforded by your efforts on the golf course, you might add two things to make our record of the day's work at Blackheath complete. First, I had the opportunity to study in some detail the club and the course which are at the centre of this villainy – for villainy I am now convinced is abroad here. Secondly, I had the opportunity to observe the man at the centre of this case, the man we agree is the projected victim, at close quarters. I might have earned my florin working for you, Watson, but I watched Alfred Bullimore also in the element where he is most at home. It was quite instructive.'

'So what next, Holmes?'

'We watch and we wait, I think.'

'You can't mean that we do nothing!'

'That is precisely what I mean, my old friend. You may inform our client that that is what we plan to do, if you think it necessary.'

'But Holmes, the man was in fear of his life when he arrived here yesterday. Having agreed to take up the case, we cannot simply –'

'It is my opinion that Alfred Bullimore is in no immediate physical danger. You may inform him of that too, if you think it will set his mind at rest; for my own part, I should not consider it necessary to do so. And now, as you say, it is time for bed.' He rose abruptly and knocked out the dottle from his pipe in the hearth.

For two weeks and more, it seemed that Holmes was right. There was no news of further developments at Blackheath. Then, as we sat down to dinner on a Wednesday evening in March, there was an impatient ringing and urgent voices at the front door of the house below us. A moment later, Mrs Hudson brought in a telegram. The message could hardly have been more stark.

It read:

PLEASE COME QUICKLY. FIRED UPON AND IN-JURED THIS AFTERNOON. ALFRED BULLIMORE.

FOUR

Not surprisingly, Alfred Bullimore looked white and drawn when we arrived at Blackheath Golf Club. It was well after dark on this March evening, but the place still seemed surprisingly quiet. The use of firearms upon people is a most serious offence, even where there is no actual loss of life, and the police treat it accordingly. I had expected urgent police activity, with a variety of people detained in the club for questioning and many uniforms in evidence around the buildings.

Instead, the club was almost deserted. A small group of members stood talking in subdued tones around the bar in the sitting-room. Bullimore led us into the Secretary's office, where a heaped fire made the room cheerful but almost oppressively warm. There was still oil lighting in this part of the club; the lamp lit the desk and the oak panelling of the room with a soft glow. It was a scene for dozing in an armchair after an excellent dinner, not for recounting the harsh and dramatic events we now had to confront.

The man at the centre of them turned and spoke as soon as I had shut the heavy oak door behind us. 'Thank you for coming so quickly, Mr Holmes. And you too, Dr Watson – or John, if I may so presume, after our game together last month.'

'Of course, Alfred. We can surely count ourselves friends, after that salutary experience,' I smiled.

'Thank you. I feel in dire need of friends at the moment, I can tell you. I don't know quite whom I can trust, even around my own golf club.' He glanced down grimly at the arm which hung uselessly at his side. It was heavily bandaged, but there was a faint red-brown stain at the centre of the whiteness, just above the elbow, on the outside part of the arm.

Holmes, never one for the social graces when there was mischief afoot, said abruptly, 'You must let Dr Watson assess the damage immediately. It might well be important to have his report available when this fellow is eventually brought to court.'

'Thank you for the thought, but that will not be necessary. The wound was dressed immediately by a doctor who is one of our members. He is not here now, but he will be prepared to describe the damage I suffered if that should prove necessary.'

'I see. Then you had better describe both the attack and its results to us now, Mr Bullimore. Please omit no detail, whether you think it important or not.' Holmes pulled a chair to within four feet of the victim, studying him as avidly as if he had been a specimen under a microscope.

It would have put me off if I had been meeting this scrutiny for the first time, but Alfred Bullimore did not seem unduly disturbed; he had said when he came to Baker Street that he had read my accounts of Holmes's earlier cases, so perhaps he had been expecting this intensity. 'The attack took place at just after five-thirty this afternoon. I was behind the main club building, on my way to see our head groundsman, Bevan. I wanted to ensure the greens were cut on Saturday morning, in preparation for the competition we have on that day.'

I said, 'It was a dull day today, but there must have been some light left at that time. Was the spot where you were attacked particularly gloomy, because –'

'Watson, we shall inspect the scene of this assault in due course. Let us first have Mr Bullimore's account of what happened, if you please.' Holmes, leaning forward towards Bullimore like a bird of prey, did not even trouble to look at me as he spoke.

The Secretary said, 'That won't take very long. The spot is indeed a dark one. There is a path behind the kitchen of the club which runs between two high banks of yew. It is no more than twelve yards long, and it is the shortest route from here to the hut where Bevan, our groundsman, has his headquarters. It was at the far end of it that I was attacked – ambushed, you might rather say.'

'Describe your assailant, please.'

'I scarcely saw him, I'm afraid. He leapt out of the bushes some five yards ahead of me. It took me a moment to realise he was pointing a pistol at me.'

'He spoke?'

'No. Not a word. He just pointed the pistol at me and fired it. I saw the muzzle spit fire in the gloom almost before I realised I was hit.'

'And you think he intended more serious damage?'

'I'm certain of it. He fired at my heart, Mr Holmes.'

'Hmmm. Then he was a very poor marksman I'd say, Mr Bullimore.'

'Or I was very lucky. I think I instinctively threw myself

sideways as he fired, but it was all over so quickly that I can't be clear just what happened.'

'Very well. You have the clothes you wore at hand?'

'I have the jacket I wore, in this cupboard. I thought you might wish to examine it.' He opened the door of a wooden locker in the corner of the room. I glimpsed stout golf shoes and a selection of gutty balls at the bottom of it before Holmes seized on the garment which hung above them.

Holmes produced his magnifying glass and examined the jagged hole in the left arm of the tweed jacket in some detail, even smelling its charred edges. Then he nodded and returned it to its hook. 'This damage was plainly inflicted at very close quarters.' He glanced down at the bandaged arm and its tell-tale centre of drying blood. 'You were lucky, as you say, Mr Bullimore. Lucky, that is, if we assume our mystery assailant was really intending to kill you.' The piercing grey eyes turned from the damaged tweed to examine the white face beside him with equal concentration.

'I'm sure he did.'

'How many shots did he fire?'

'Only the one.'

'Have you any idea why? I'm assuming any villain who meant business would be carry a modern automatic pistol.'

'No. I hadn't even thought about that. But I see what you mean. Perhaps he thought he'd killed me with the first effort. Or perhaps he thought I was going to attack him. That was my first impulse, before I realised he was pointing a weapon at me; I probably made some sort of lunge towards him.'

I decided that it was time I re-entered the conversation; I had not spoken since Holmes's brusque dismissal of my thoughts on the location of this outrage. 'It may be that the fellow was fearful of discovery, that when he realised that he had only winged you he was afraid that you would recognise him. That might indicate that he is someone well known to you.'

Holmes smiled indulgently. 'It might indicate a whole variety of things, Watson. The most obvious would be that whoever fired that weapon did not intend a mortal wound. However, Mr Bullimore is certain that he did. It is time, I think, for us to inspect the scene of the crime.'

As he turned towards the door, I said, 'Let us pause for just a minute, please. You should tell us now what the police think of all this, Alfred. Are they combing the area in search of your assailant? Have they informed you whether they think as I do that the culprit comes from somewhere within the club?'

Bullimore had been about to follow Holmes out of his office. Now he turned back to me. I saw that he looked embarrassed, despite his pallor. 'The police have not been informed, Dr Watson. I am content that the matter should rest with Sherlock Holmes, and I have persuaded the few club members who were around at the time of the attack that this is the best course from the point of view of the Blackheath Golf Club. No one wants lurid publicity for the club, least of all me.'

It was time, I thought to make a stand. 'That is very unselfish, but surely very unwise as well. No one is a greater admirer of the abilities of my colleague than I am, but the police have resources we cannot duplicate. In the case of a serious crime like this, they will bring in a team of men. They have access to the records of the criminal fraternity. They will know the proven villains in the area, will probably even know those with access to firearms. You are being reckless with your own safety: I must urge you in the strongest possible terms to –'

'If the gentleman is content to rely on our humble resources, to put his fate in our hands, you should not dissuade him, Watson. You have seen at close hand the efforts of our friends the police; indeed you have recorded some of their bumbling alongside my modest successes. I am surprised you still display such a touching faith in their efficiency.'

I took a deep breath. 'Holmes, I must put this bluntly, since you force me to do so. At times you are confident to the point of arrogance. A little over two weeks ago, you told me that in your opinion Mr Bullimore was in no physical danger. Today he has been fortunate to escape with his life. This is no time to let personal vanity interfere with sound judgement. I think the police should be informed of this attack without further delay. By all means continue with your independent investigation, but –'

'Very well! You have made your point, Watson. It carries a certain logic, though I cannot agree with it. Let us leave the decision to the victim. Mr Bullimore, in the light of my friend's comments, do you now wish to reconsider your decision and bring in the full might of the police force?'

Bullimore looked into each of our faces in turn. 'No. I agreed with the members that we would not bring in the police, and I shall stick to that agreement. I have full confidence in Mr Holmes, whatever you say about his under-estimating the danger.'

Holmes smiled that annoying smile which said that he had known what the decision would be, then said, 'Then let us delay no longer in examining the scene of this assault.' He wheeled imperiously towards the door and indicated that Bullimore should lead the way with a wide sweep of his arm.

We followed the route through the clubhouse which Bullimore had taken a few hours earlier. It led us down a corridor which passed the kitchen door. I saw the chef, Marcel Lebrun, watching us as we went. His scowling face was full of hostility. His work must now be finished for the night, for the dining-room was deserted; I wondered if he had stayed in his kitchen solely to review developments as Sherlock Holmes took up the case. In due course, we should have to talk to this fellow, I was sure.

It was gloomy outside, with low clouds moving swiftly across a slim crescent of moon. At first, I thought that we would be able to do no more than establish the precise spot where the attack had taken place, but Holmes produced a bull's-eye lamp and turned its shaft of light upon the yews. The sudden channel of white light seemed quite brilliant after the darkness. It was a dismal spot with the tall club-house cutting out the light behind and the straggling yews fringing a path no more than four feet wide. It must have been cheerless here even at midday.

Holmes made the victim stand as near as possible to the spot where he had been hit, whilst he himself shuffled back and forth under Bullimore's instructions until he was in the position the would-be assassin had chosen. He insisted that Bullimore be as precise as possible about the spot, and about the route his attacker had taken to escape. I felt quite sorry for the Secretary, who showed increasing tension as he was made to re-live a moment which must have been quite horrific, but I had seen Holmes at work before at the scenes of crimes and I knew his methods.

We spent a good fifteen minutes in that Stygian place, with only the rapidly shifting beam of Holmes's torch to guide us. I was almost as relieved as Bullimore when we moved along the path to the head groundsman's hut, which had been the Secretary's goal on his ill-fated journey a few hours earlier. All here was locked and barred at this hour, of course. It struck me how easy it would have been for someone from here or the professional's and caddiemaster's sheds which adjoined it to have perpetrated this outrage. Anyone from this area could have waited for the Secretary, shot him, and been back at his place of work by the time people arrived to investigate. Or he could have left the premises altogether, of course; the quiet road which ran alongside the course was no more than forty yards away through the bushes, as Alfred Bullimore ruefully conceded to us.

We went back into the deserted clubhouse, where Holmes decided that there was nothing more to be done until the morrow. Bullimore looked all in by this time; no doubt the loss of blood and delayed shock, which I had noted often before in cases of sudden injury, were now affecting even as robust a constitution as his. 'If there is no one here to accompany you, then you must let us see you home. You cannot risk a faint with no one to minister to you,' I said.

'Of course we must deliver the victim safely to his home,' said my companion with alacrity. 'We have presumed upon your injured state for far too long already, Mr Bullimore.'

He pulled out his cab whistle from beneath his cape and bustled away into the darkness. I heard the faint sound of the single long blast which would summon a four-wheeler, and he came back into the Secretary's office a few minutes later to announce that our conveyance was waiting outside. It was a kindness in Holmes which I was happy to see after his earlier brusque concentration on the essentials of the investigation.

Yet I might have known that it was not merely humane consideration which drove this unique man. Whilst we waited for a moment in the carriage for Bullimore to join us, Holmes whispered, 'One may find out much by an investigation of the domicile and the domestic circumstances of those involved in crime. That applies to victims as much as to suspects, Watson. An investigation of Bullimore's domestic circumstances – about which he has so far been singularly reticent – may give some indication not only of his way of life but of persons who may wish to attack him.' He produced the deerstalker hat he favoured when we were out of town, pulled it down firmly about his ears and settled himself contentedly back within the folds of his cape.

He was right about Bullimore being reluctant to allow us into his everyday life away from the golf club. He looked thoroughly exhausted when he joined us in the brougham, but when we had completed the short journey to his house, he did not want us to go into it with him. After my brief conversation with Holmes about the matter, I was determined that we should do so. 'Really, my dear fellow, you must allow a medical man to know what is the best course in these circumstances,' I said firmly. 'You have lost a considerable amount of blood – no one can be sure how much – and your whole constitution is more shaken than you realise yourself at this moment. I should not be happy, indeed I should be professionally irresponsible, if I did not see you safely into bed for a good night's rest.'

Holmes looked into the wan face of our companion and said sardonically, 'You had much better accede to Dr Watson's prescription, you know. He can be quite boringly insistent at times like this, when he thinks he is preserving health.'

Bullimore said gruffly, 'Very well. I am stronger than either of you seems to think, but if it will satisfy you to see me safely stowed between the sheets, then by all means come in. But don't expect to find the place tidy!'

It was a high, narrow house in a quiet terrace, and despite his warning the interior was neat and orderly. It was the neatness perhaps of an occupant who spent little time at home rather than one who was obsessively tidy, but it was a pleasant enough place. The drawing-room smelt a little musty as we entered and, with no fire in the grate, the place was cold. I said I wanted to see its occupant ready for bed before we left, and he left us with the decanter of whisky and disappeared up the stairs; we heard him presently disrobing above our heads.

It gave us the opportunity Holmes had desired to look at the room where the occupant spent most of his time in the house. There were two water-colours and a small oil just inside the door, but the only photograph in the room was a stiffly posed portrait of a balding man standing erect beside a portly matron, who was seated beside a round table with an aspidistra plant upon it. Holmes examined the fading sepia and declared that it was around twenty years old. These looked like the parents of Alfred Bullimore.

I confess I had hoped to see the photograph of a younger woman. In my wilder imaginings I had even thought there might be a portrait of the fair Mrs Ross, who assisted the Secretary in his duties at the golf club and possibly favoured him in other ways, but of her or any other young woman there was no sign. I told myself stubbornly that this might be merely caution, that any picture of Mrs Ross would surely be concealed in the more intimate recesses of the bedroom upstairs.

Apart from one factor, this living area was singularly unrevealing about the life of its owner. The room was dominated by the sport which we already knew was Bullimore's ruling passion. Three walls were dotted with paintings of various golf courses. The fourth was the most interesting. The mantelpiece over the empty fireplace was crowded with the trophies he had won, each with a neat hand-written card beneath it giving the details of the particular triumph. The wall above them was covered with sketches and paintings of the great men in the history of the game – old Tom Morris and his son; Willie Park and his; the great amateur Open champions, John Ball and Harold Hilton. Two larger drawings hung supreme over all. They were of the current Open champion (we were still in early 1896), J.H. Taylor, and his great rival professional, Harry Vardon.

When Alfred Bullimore re-entered the room in his dressing gown and saw me studying these, he was suddenly re-animated. He was prepared to enlarge upon the splendours of Taylor's golf in winning the Opens of 1894 and

1895, but Holmes cut him short with a peremptory enquiry about the identity of the people in the room's single photograph. Bullimore, plainly disappointed to be diverted from his discourse upon golf, confirmed that these were indeed his parents, though they had both now been dead for some years.

'I must insist now that you get some rest, Alfred,' I said. 'Mr Holmes has confirmed that he will wish to speak to various people at Blackheath Golf Club tomorrow, but there is no need for you to be present. I will attend here and dress your wound for you if you wish it, but I know you have your own physician and I must not trespass upon his territory.'

'Thank you. I do not think your ministrations will be necessary. No doubt Dr Bowen, who gave me such prompt attention at the club, will be prepared to deal with the wound, as you say, but I fancy I shall not need much in the way of treatment. I was really very lucky, you know, very lucky indeed. I believe that after a good night's rest, I shall be able to attend to my duties at the club tomorrow. Indeed, I hope it will not be very long before I am playing again!' He smiled and looked at the portraits on the wall, the fingers of his right hand straying automatically towards the bandage on his left.

There was a protracted silence as Holmes and I rode home in the brougham. It was late, but it was not just fatigue which kept us silent; each of us was busy with his own thoughts. We were crossing Waterloo Bridge, with the moonlight gleaming faintly on the dark waters of the Thames below us, before I said, 'Bullimore is a brave man, no doubt. I admire his wish to avoid placing his golf club at the centre of a scandal. But he really should have brought the police into this, you know, Holmes, however much his faith in you flatters your vanity.'

There was such a long pause that I thought for a moment that my companion had fallen asleep. Then a voice from the darkness said, 'You are wrong on two counts, Watson. Alfred Bullimore was right to keep the police out of this. But I don't believe he has any great faith in the powers of Sherlock Holmes. We shall have to show him that we can get to the heart of this business.'

FIVE

Holmes was impatient for me to complete my breakfast on the next morning. I tried to do justice to Mrs Hudson's ham and eggs, but it was difficult when I was so aware of the hovering presence beside the table. I suspected that my companion had eaten almost nothing himself; it was his custom to starve himself when applying his mind to the central puzzle of a case. But after years of experience, I knew better than to remonstrate with him about the habit.

There was a bitter east wind swirling round the long, low buildings of the clubhouse when we arrived at Blackheath. It was definitely a morning to be indoors, but Holmes insisted on inspecting again the scene of the previous day's atrocity. 'We shall have the benefit of daylight for our scrutiny,' he said, his long, thin nose sniffing the bitter gusts with eager anticipation, 'though there will assuredly be little enough light even now in that wretched place.'

He was right in one sense. The place was gloomy and shaded, as well as piercingly cold; I doubt if the sun ever shone into this particular corner. It was certainly a spot well chosen for an ambush. I said as much to Holmes as I rubbed my gloved hands vigorously together. 'The choice of place argues someone who knows the territory well,' I said. 'If I were choosing to shoot someone and get away without arrest, this would be the very best position in the area.'

'Agreed. Lend me your penknife for a moment, please, Watson.' He examined the place where Bullimore had fallen, lined it up with the place where his attacker had waited, then disappeared for a few moments beneath the branches of the straggling yews. I heard a small cry of satisfaction, and he emerged a moment later with his left hand in his jacket pocket. I knew he had found something, but he refused to show it to me. 'It is of no great importance at this stage,' he said. 'It may not even be connected with last night's incident. I shall know more when I get it under the microscope tonight.'

I put my penknife back into my pocket when he handed it to me, refusing to appear curious about his find. I said stubbornly, 'I still think the fact that the assailant obviously knows this territory well may be the most important thing of all.'

'Let us agree that some local knowledge is likely in the one who perpetrated last night's events,' said Holmes. But he was already on one knee, examining the ground where Bullimore had fallen. 'The ground is generally too dry for our purposes, after the east winds of the last few days. But this path between the yews is so shaded that the surface has remained soft enough to tell us a little. You can see where Bullimore entered the path, where he stopped suddenly when confronted; we can be sure that these are the sole marks of his shoes, for I took care to examine them last night.'

It was true enough; indeed, I saw it plainly, once Holmes had pointed it out to me, but I doubt if I should have discovered it so confidently if I had been alone. Unfortunately, we were not so lucky with the attacker. He had stood at the end of a short path between the straggling yews, and many other feet must have passed that way. There were faint traces of foot marks at the spot where the gunman had stood, but nothing we could decide were definitely his traces. It was frustrating that we could find nothing which might help us to identify the attacker, but of course Bullimore had been stopped at the darkest and gloomiest point of the path, where it was wettest. Moreover, thanks to Holmes's close observation on the previous evening, we knew exactly what shoes the victim had been wearing, and the Secretary was a powerfully built man of considerable weight.

'Ah, Watson, that is good. You have learned some discernment over the years. What then do you deduce from the inconclusive collection of marks around where this mysterious attacker stood?'

I thought for a moment, then brightened. 'The gunman was not heavily built like Bullimore, or he would have left more evidence of his presence behind him. A small, light, fellow, then. Even a child, perhaps – but surely a child would have been unlikely to have access to a firearm.'

'Quite so, Watson.' Holmes was on his knees now, with his glass out to study the ground beneath the last of the yews. 'You have omitted one possibility, of course.'

It took a moment for the realisation to dawn. 'Good God! A woman, you mean.'

'I mean nothing, Watson. I am simply encouraging you to complete the logic of your deduction. If you think a lightly built man and a child are possibilities, then you must plainly also countenance a woman.' He scrambled to his feet. 'It is no good; there is nothing recent discernible here other than the paw marks of rabbits.'

I nodded regretfully, for I could discern nothing either. 'Nothing more that is useful then. Still, we have established that we must consider that this foul attack might even have been the work of a woman.'

'And it may be that in due course the tracks of those rabbits may prove the most significant marks of all!' Holmes whirled round and strode into the groundsman's shed behind him. 'Mr David Bevan, I believe,' he said to the rather apprehensive man who stood with his cap in his hands. 'Sherlock Holmes and Dr Watson. Pray tell us what you can of this strange business, which took place so close to you.'

Bevan was a squat figure, with the hard muscles of a man who spent long days in physical activity. His grizzled hair was thinning, and he had a scar on his cheek which made him look more sinister than he sounded when he spoke. 'I was in here when it happened. It must have been about half past five last night. We'd finished work on the course for the day because it was almost dark; I was in here on my own, sharpening the blade of that scythe over there, ready for the spring growth.' In the corner of the hut, we could see the long, bright blade of the implement he spoke of. 'I knew nothing until I heard the shot. Even then, it took me a moment to realise what it was – I could scarcely believe my ears, if you see what I mean.'

'We do, Mr Bevan. But describe to us exactly what you heard. Take your time, for it may be important.'

'Well, I heard nothing before the shot. There might have been noise, mind you, but I was busy with my sharpening stone on the blade of yon scythe.'

'Did you hear Mr Bullimore shout?'

'Yes. Almost at the same time as the shot. May have been just before, but I couldn't be sure of that. Then, afterwards, there was a long cry of pain, and I think he said, "I'm hit!"'

'Good, Bevan! So far, very good!' Holmes, who had wandered across to inspect the scythe, now whirled upon his witness. 'And what did you hear from the assailant?'

'Nothing, sir. I've asked myself that through the night, but I'm sure he never spoke, or if he did, it must have been before the shot, when I was busy with my sharpening stone.'

'Very well. What did you see, then? Presumably you went straight out to see what had happened?'

'Yes, sir. Well, pretty straight, that is. I grabbed that mallet you see on the bench there. All I'd heard was a shot, see. I didn't know then that it was our Secretary that was hurt. My first thought that it was some villains who'd wandered in from the road outside here, nothing to do with the club. If there were guns about, I wanted to protect myself.'

'Very wise of you. So there was a second or two's delay. No more?'

'No more than that, sir. And as soon as I opened the door, I heard Mr Bullimore groaning and shouting for help, so I went straight to him.'

'Did anyone pass you? Did you hear the sound of anyone in the bushes as you went to Mr Bullimore's aid?'

'No, sir. No one passed me, I'm sure of that, and I didn't hear any movements in the undergrowth. I was bred in the country, the son of a gamekeeper, and I be pretty sure I'd have caught the sound of anyone moving away through the bushes. Of course, he might have been there, Mr Holmes, quiet like, watching me lift Mr Bullimore and help him to the clubhouse. I've thought of that, and it fair made my blood run cold, I can tell you.'

'No doubt it would. But you're sure you can tell us nothing of the gunman's escape, when his likely route must have taken him within yards of you?'

'I am sure of that, sir. But it wasn't his only route, was it? Not at that time: it was almost dark, and the back of the clubhouse was deserted. He could have gone that way safely enough, and seen his way more clearly than past my hut. Or he could even . . .'

Bevan's speech came to a sudden stop. He stood looking at the earthen floor of his hut and twisting his cap violently between his hands. Holmes laughed – that short, excited laugh which burst from him when he had the scent of detection in his nostrils. 'You're right, of course! David Bevan, you should have been a policeman! I'll say it for you: he could even have gone into the clubhouse. Or to express the idea completely, he could even have gone *back* into the clubhouse. Yes, that is a possibility. A very definite one, as you are sure that he didn't go past your hut. But don't worry, I shall not convey to the members or staff within the building that you were bold enough to suggest the idea. Thank you for your help: you will make a good witness, if it should ever come to that. Come, Watson.'

In the clubhouse, we met an unexpected figure. Alfred Bullimore, still white-faced but otherwise seemingly almost himself, was waiting for us on the parquet floor of the hall-way. When I rebuked him for his presence and said that he should be at home resting, he brushed aside the suggestion.

'I have got away with it quite amazingly, Dr Watson. The arm has been cleaned and dressed this morning and has only a flesh wound. The bullet merely nicked me – didn't even damage the muscle tissue of the arm. It seems I'll be playing golf again in a day or two. That is just as well, with the season beginning in less than a month! Anyway, I'd rather the fellow who shot me saw me back at work here than skulking at home.'

This was a bravado I did not feel happy about; he was vulnerable here, as his assailant had already amply demonstrated. 'You really should have the police in on this,' I said irritably. Brave man he might be, but I was beginning to lose patience with Alfred Bullimore and his unashamed obsession with golf.

'I have confidence in Sherlock Holmes, and the members prefer that this matter is kept out of the news sheets for as long as possible. It is a difficult task I have set you, Mr Holmes, I know, but I shall do whatever I can to facilitate your enquiries. To that end, I have compiled a list of the people you might wish to see here. I thought we could see them together in my office; I have had extra chairs put in there for you and Dr Watson.'

Holmes glanced at the scrap of paper. 'We shall need to see most of these people, certainly. But your list is not comprehensive. And we shall not see them with you, Mr Bullimore. Most of these names are members of your staff . . . your presence would certainly inhibit the candour which we strive to achieve.'

Bullimore was put out by his exclusion, but he saw the point. In the end, we did not even use his office, since we agreed with him that the normal routine of the club should be disturbed as little as possible. He found us a store room at the rear of the building; within ten minutes, we had a fire burning in the little-used grate and had replaced dusty cupboards and tables with chairs and a desk. I tried to install Holmes behind this, but he took one of the armchairs by the fire and set me at the desk with my notebook.

Because they were in the club – indeed they seemed habitually to be so – we saw first the two members I had met when I came to play golf in the previous month. Herbert Robinson, the first of these, had little to contribute. He was a heavily built man: had he come to me in my professional capacity I should have had to tell him that he was seriously overweight. His collar seemed rather tight, so that his neck bulged beneath a florid face and bulbous eyes. In view of his weight, it was most unlikely that he would be the villain who had held the pistol on the previous day, but he was such an habitué of the place that he might well have opinions on the source of this crime. 'Bullimore's doing the right thing, letting you chaps look into this,' he said as he sat down heavily, looking with distaste at the dusty walls of this disused room. 'Don't want those damned peelers stamping round the place, do we?'

I said, 'He is a brave man, Alfred Bullimore. But foolhardy, in my opinion. Do you know anything about what happened yesterday?'

'No. I was here all right, but the first I knew about it was the commotion when we heard poor old Bullimore being brought back into the club. That fellow Bevan was helping him in. Greenkeepers shouldn't come into the club at all, of course, but I suppose the circumstances were a bit exceptional. Ironical that it should be Bevan who had to help our Secretary really.'

Holmes had been smiling his way through the man's bumbling discourse, prepared I think to get rid of him swiftly. Now that long nose sniffed something of interest and he snapped, 'And why should it be strange that Bevan was at hand to help? His headquarters make him the nearest person to the place of the incident – apart from the gunman, of course.'

'Oh, nothing strange about that. I said ironic and that is what I meant. Bevan being the man who had been threatened with unemployment by Bullimore. I expect he told you about it, when you went in to see him this morning.'

This fellow wasn't entirely the self-satisfied bumbler I had supposed. He knew how we had spent our morning thus far; no doubt not much else that went on in Blackheath Golf Club escaped him. Holmes glanced at me and I said, 'Why was your Secretary proposing to get rid of Bevan?'

'Not for anything he'd done. Course always seems in pretty fair condition to me; greens have certainly improved under Bevan. But he's older than he looks – nearly sixty, I think. Bullimore had the idea we should bring in another man as head of the ground staff. Keep Bevan on under someone else's direction, on a reduced salary. He said we'd still have his skills and experience available, at less money.'

In those days, long before we had trade unions established in most trades, you could do more or less what you wanted with staff, but it seemed harsh treatment of a man who had apparently given good service. Bevan had not mentioned his grievance to us: I wondered how significant that omission might be.

Perhaps Herbert Robinson followed our thoughts, for he added, 'I don't suppose Bevan was happy about the idea, but I don't see him taking pot-shots at the Secretary because of it, do you?'

Holmes bestowed upon him a quick, mirthless smile. 'No, I don't, Mr Robinson. But you see our problem; it is discovering anyone who might take such extreme measures. With your wide knowledge of the members of the club, perhaps you can tell us of people who disliked its Secretary strongly enough to take a revolver to him.'

'Steady on, now. I wouldn't say Bullimore was a very popular chap, but –'

'And why not, would you say? He is a fine golfer and seems an efficient enough manager of the club's resources. Why then is he not more popular?'

Robinson looked as if he wished he had not embarked upon this, but Holmes, sitting forward now on the edge of his chair, was not to be denied. The plump man stumbled into an explanation, 'Well, he's a bit full of himself, you see. Bit arrogant, I suppose. He's very much taken up with his own golf and how he can improve it. We all know he's the best player in the club by far, and we applaud his successes in open competitions, but there are times when it seems he could be a lot more tolerant of other people's problems.'

I stifled a smile at the picture this conjured up of this plump and ageing man toiling along the course behind an unsympathetic Alfred Bullimore.

'And there are people who say he's always out on the course, not attending to the needs of members around the club as a good secretary should. But he's only an Hon.

Sec., so you can't expect blood, can you? And dash it all, these aren't grounds for trying to shoot a chap down, are they?'

'Indeed they aren't, Mr Robinson,' said Holmes. 'I fancy we shall have to delve much deeper before we find what is really at the bottom of this business. Thank you for your help. Perhaps you would be good enough to send in Mr Frobisher now.' My friend spoke abruptly and stared hard into the fire. I had to get up and open the door for Robinson before he realised that he had been dismissed.

Edward Frobisher was as lean as Robinson had been plump. He had sharp features and quick brown eyes, which darted inquisitively round this room he had never seen before. He also had a lawyer's caution: yes, it might be fair to say that Bullimore was not universally popular; no, he knew of no one who would feel resentment strong enough to make him resort to firearms. 'That would need a pretty desperate fellow, wouldn't you say?'

'I should indeed. Or a desperate woman, of course.' I thought I detected a little start in the man who sat on the other side of the fire as Holmes said this, but he gave no other sign of surprise. Holmes, forced to set his own hare running, said softly, 'There is one lady, of course, who is in almost daily contact with the victim of this shooting.'

'Mrs Ross, yes. She is a respectable widow. If you are suggesting –'

Holmes held up a hand. 'I suggest nothing, Mr Frobisher. I merely point out that an assault with a firearm requires no physical strength and could thus be achieved as easily by a woman as by the most obvious blackguard. What was the occupation of the late Mr Ross?'

'He was an army officer, I believe. A captain. Died of typhus, in India, I think.'

'Hmm! Army officers are issued with pistols. I wonder if the late Captain Ross's pistol was ever returned to the regimental arsenal.'

'Look here, Holmes, if you're going to go around offering speculations like that, I should warn you that —'

'A thought cast upon the air among the three of us, Mr Frobisher, that is all. I trust that it will go no further than this room. And it goes without saying that any similar speculations you make here will be treated as equally confidential.'

'I don't care to speculate. I'm a lawyer.' He did not seem to detect any irony in that.

'Would you say that Mr Bullimore is popular with the members at large?'

Frobisher frowned irritably, and I thought for a moment that he might say that the proposition was much too wide and vague for a lawyer to entertain it. Instead, he said with some reluctance, 'He is not a popular man, no. It is not easy to say why. Perhaps it is because of his general bearing and his insensitivity to the feelings of others. He gives the impression that he has little idea of the effect some of his statements will have on people. Sometimes he does not even seem to care about such things. But I do not know of anyone with a particular grievance against the man strong enough to develop into the real hate which must surely have informed this latest outrage.'

A cool, intelligent man, this, I decided. One who weighed his words carefully before he spoke and did think of their effects upon others. Holmes said quietly, 'I believe you thought at one time that you might become Secretary of the club yourself.'

Frobisher had plainly not expected this. He glanced furiously at me, but I took care to be writing diligent notes upon my paper at the desk. 'I don't know where you got that information from, but it is accurate. I think most of the members wanted me to take over, before Bullimore came along and offered himself.' He spoke the name with real contempt, and one had the impression for the first time of a mask dropping away. But Frobisher gathered himself quickly in the pause which followed. 'It is not a paid post, of course – I should not have been interested in it if it had been. But it is an honour among gentlemen to be asked to be their Secretary. I had done a certain amount of legal work gratis for the club, and I think most people assumed that I would become Secretary when our previous incumbent retired from the office. But Bullimore dazzled with his golf and canvassed a few influential people in the club; it was enough to secure himself the appointment. It was a disappointment to me, but it was three years ago and now it matters not.'

It seemed to me by his pinched mouth and his staring resolutely ahead of him that it mattered a great deal. But we couldn't draw him further upon the subject. He said evenly that he supposed Alfred Bullimore was a perfectly competent Secretary: the course was in excellent order and the clubhouse was run well enough. Most of the members were probably quite satisfied. He was a lawyer again, fencing defensively under cross-examination, and we were plainly going to get nothing further from him.

'An interesting man, with much more bubbling beneath

the surface than he allows the world to see,' was Holmes's opinion of him.

'And a man cool enough and with nerve enough to have stood behind a pistol,' was mine.

We saw the chef, Marcel Lebrun, next. He was a short man with a very black moustache, much given to a Gallic use of the shoulders; indeed, he tried to shrug away many of our questions. He was not fluent in English, but I suspected that for some of the time he was using his difficulty as a tactic to give him time to assess our enquiries. Finally, Holmes asked him directly what he thought of the Secretary.

He shrugged again. 'Mr Bullimore is not a likeable man.'

'He does not treat you well?'

Another heave of the shoulders: it was almost an automatic prelude to his answers. 'He treats me well enough. But I am a good chef; he knows I could go elsewhere.'

'And you would earn more in a London hotel, no doubt.'

He glared at Holmes, who returned his stare equably enough. 'I would work there much harder. I like it here. And I have my accommodation.'

'You live on the premises?'

'I have two rooms, yes. Above my kitchen. My living-room looks out over the golf course. Is very nice.'

'I see. And you don't like Mr Bullimore very much, do you?'

Again the resentment smouldered beneath his expressive black eyebrows. 'Is all right, I suppose. He lets me get on with my job in the kitchen.' He looked around the room in the pause which followed. Then he said unexpectedly, 'Mr Bullimore, he does not treat women well. Is nothing to do with me, but I do not like it.'

We pressed him on this, but he shook his head as well as his shoulders this time. 'I no say more. I say too much already. You ask him, if you want more. But you do not tell him what I said.' He got to his feet and shambled towards the door without being dismissed.

Holmes let him set his hand upon the handle of the door before he said, 'Where were you at the time of this shooting, Monsieur Lebrun?'

He whirled like a hunted man at that. 'I am in my kitchen. I hear nothing. I know nothing – not until Bullimore is brought back into his office do I know.'

'Can anyone confirm this?'

'No. I am alone there at the time. But I did not shoot this man, even though I do not like him.'

We had to let him go with that. I said to Holmes, 'That man is hiding something. I don't know what, but I don't trust him. I think we should search his rooms. I should not be surprised if we found the pistol there.'

Holmes smiled. 'And do we search the house of David Bevan? Of Edward Frobisher? We can't just select the foreigners around the place, you know, Watson. We are not the police, thank the Lord – we do not have their powers of search. We have to proceed by more subtle means. Besides, I suspect even you might shrink from searching the home of our next witness.'

'Why? Who's next?'

'A subject to gladden the heart of an impressionable chap like you, Watson. And a name significantly omitted from Alfred Bullimore's list of people he thought we should see. The fair Mrs Ross.'

'I'll go and get her.'

'No, Watson, stay here. In fact, have my chair by the fire and question her yourself. Your well-known charm with the ladies may elicit more from her than my direct approach. I shall go and fetch her here for you; I look forward to seeing Alfred Bullimore's reaction.' He laid his cape across the desk and was gone before I could protest.

I was not used to questioning people involved in our cases. I had done it of course, as when Holmes sent me down alone to the home of the Baskervilles on Dartmoor, but when Holmes was with me I was normally thrust into a secondary role, which suited me well enough. Now, in that small, increasingly warm room, with its one high window, I felt that I as well as Mrs Ross was being assessed and dissected by that piercing gaze from behind the desk.

The lady wore a soft grey velvet dress which matched exactly the colour of her eyes. It was entirely becoming, though it was not the garb of the typists who were at that time becoming common in city offices. But I was and am no expert in the practicalities of female clothing. In any case, Mrs Christobel Ross worked only for two hours on three mornings a week in the club, so the purchase of special clothes for this work might have been deemed an extravagance. She had regular features, rounded enough to remove any severity, and a complexion as soft and smooth as the surface of a ripe peach. The effect of these attributes was in no way diminished by the slight frown of anxiety which furrowed her forehead as Holmes ushered her into the room.

'Do sit down, Mrs Ross. This shouldn't take us very long.' Conscious of a most annoying smile on the face of my colleague behind the desk, I shifted my armchair to point a little more towards the blazing fire, in an attempt to cut him out of my vision.

'I don't think I can help you much. But if I can – well, of course we're all only too anxious to clear up this awful business. I still cannot believe it! It seems that this man who has been threatening Mr Bullimore for months has begun trying to kill him now.'

'Yes. It must be very distressing for you to come into the club and find such things have been happening. But there has been a gradual build-up towards this violence. Would you tell us what you remember of that, please, Mrs Ross.'

'Yes. Well, there were the letters first of course.'

'You saw them?'

'Some of them, yes. I think Alfr – Mr Bullimore – destroyed the earliest ones because he didn't wish to alarm me. When I did see the later ones, I didn't like them. He said I shouldn't take them so seriously, that they were the work of a crank with a grudge and nothing would come of them. But I was right to be alarmed about them, wasn't I?'

'It certainly seems so now, yes. That is if we assume that it was the man who wrote them who took the shot at Mr Bullimore, and there seems little reason to doubt that. Can you remember what the messages said?'

'Not exactly. Mr Bullimore destroyed them, you see, tried to laugh them off when he saw that I was alarmed. But I remember that the first ones were pretty vague. Then they became more personal, and began to centre upon Alfred himself.'

This time she was too late to correct her use of her employer's first name. She looked down at her small feet and blushed slowly. As with many beautiful women, every action she took seemed to become her. I heard Holmes softly repeating the words "became more personal . . ." as he affected to write at the desk. I said softly, 'And what about the style of these missives? Can you recall anything about the ink and the handwriting, Mrs Ross?'

'They were printed in block capitals. In black ink. They looked almost as though the fellow had used a ruler on the straight strokes.'

Exactly like the sample we had seen, which had finally alarmed Bullimore enough to send him racing to Baker Street. 'And what about the way these wretched things were delivered? Did they come through the post?' Holmes should be proud of my objectivity, I thought: I was allowing the lady the chance to contradict Bullimore's account of these things.

So far she had corroborated his story at every point, and she now continued to do so. 'No, none of the ones I saw came by post. I'm not here for most of the deliveries, of course, but I saw some of the envelopes, and none of them were stamped. Most of them were put in the office for Mr Bullimore to find.'

'And none of them arrived when you were working there?'
'No.'

'You realise this makes it more likely that our villain is someone who has access to the club and knows the comings and goings of its secretary? It might be an employee of the club, perhaps, or even one of the members.'

She shuddered, and I thought for a moment that she was going to weep. Instead she looked from me to the fire and said, 'I am sure that most of the people employed here are entirely trustworthy. I'm certain none of them hates Alfred enough to try to kill him.'

'Are you saying that this is the work of one of the members?' For a moment, I was excited by the thought that she had someone definitely in mind for the crime of the previous night. 'You can rely on us to respect any confidence, Mrs Ross. But if you have even a suspicion that any –'

'I have not.' The soft voice rang out clearly and decisively in that small, still room. 'I was merely defending the people that I see as my colleagues after working here for the last eighteen months. I repeat only what I said just now: I shall be extremely surprised if this business ends in the arrest of anyone who works for Blackheath Golf Club.'

'That shows a commendable loyalty. But I'm sure you wish to see this villain caught before he does serious harm to Mr Bullimore.' She had still not looked back into my face and she did not do so now, even to confirm this. I said, 'Forgive me, but there can be no secrets in a situation like this. You have twice referred to your direct employer here by his Christian name. Am I right in presuming that you are closer to Mr Bullimore than would be implied by what is merely a working relationship?'

Mrs Ross looked me full in the face at last, blushing furiously. The soft grey eyes flashed bright with temper, so that I had a sudden vision of what this demure and lovely woman might do when roused. I thought she was going to flare out at me. Instead, after a silence charged with emotion, she looked back into the fire and said flatly, 'You phrase the question with all the delicacy I could expect, Dr Watson. You are a decent man, I believe.'

'Then you must see that the question requires an answer.'

'I suppose it does. Despite what you might think, I have little experience of these matters. Yes, I cared for Alfred, and I believed he cared for me. I was lonely when I came here. My husband had been dead two years; I was alone in a place where I had no friends; I had had no conversation save that of a small child for months before I came to work here.'

She enunciated these things as though ticking them off on a list she had gone over many times in private to account for her actions. I said gently, 'There is no reason why you should not have cared for the man who gave you work here.'

'No. And for a time, I believed that he cared for me.'

I glanced at Holmes, who was sitting at the desk with his chin sunk upon his chest, and received the tiny nod which told me he wanted me to pursue this. I said, 'Forgive me, Mrs Ross, but –'

'Thank you for addressing me as Mrs Ross. There are some who would be less polite.'

She smiled a bitter smile at the fire, as if by her conduct she had forsaken all the rights which might have belonged to a lady.

'I call you only by your proper title, Mrs Ross, and need no thanks for that. But you are an intelligent woman, and you must see that in these desperate circumstances, we need to know the details of –'

'You mean that I am a suspect in this affair! That I might have tried to kill Alfred Bullimore! That you would like to know where I was when that shot was fired.'

'I mean that we should like some account of your relationship with the man who has been the victim of a violent and cowardly attack, Mrs Ross.'

She glanced at me again. A wry smile stole over her full lips as she said, 'You must be good with difficult patients, Dr Watson. You are handling this very well. I am lucky to be accounting for myself to you rather than to some insensitive policeman. Very well, I shall tell you then; I was lonely, even a little desperate, I suppose, when I came here. To have some adult company on three mornings a week was more important to me than the money I received, though any small supplement to the pension received by an officer's widow is useful. Naturally, I saw more of Alfred Bullimore than of anyone else. He was kind and considerate, and appreciative of the work I did in the office.'

She stopped there, and eventually I prompted, 'And in time, the relationship developed into something more serious.'

'How delicate you are, Dr.' A bitter laugh, wrenched from some inner depth of pain. 'That happened in a very short time, when I look back upon it now. I see now how vulnerable I was at that time. I shall not be so again. Alfred has taught me that, at any rate. Yes, our relationship "developed into something more serious", as you kindly put it. I felt deeply for him, and he said he felt deeply about me. I believed that we would be married, after a decent interval of courtship.'

'But that is not going to happen.'

'No!' I had never heard such a wealth of hate explode into that simple monosyllable. It rang round the room almost like a pistol shot, I thought, though Holmes would no doubt take me to task for expressing it so dramatically.

'Alfred said he cared deeply for me, but it is not so. He cares deeply only for golf. I know it sounds ridiculous to say that about a mere game – the reaction of a woman who has been spurned, you will no doubt say. But it is true. Alfred Bullimore is a fanatic about golf. Nothing must come in the way of his progress in the game. Other people as well as I have found that to be so, though none at so heavy a cost as I. Perhaps it is his obsession with golf which has led him into this danger – don't ask me to say why, because I cannot. But I have seen his passion for the game, and I know it is unhealthy.'

It was a ridiculous proposition, and I think she knew it. But she spoke with such intensity in that quiet, still room that her conviction blazed as bright as the flames of the fire in the grate. She was looking at those flames as Holmes said quietly from the desk behind her, 'Where were you at five-thirty last night, Mrs Ross?'

There was no start of outrage from the woman in grey velvet, no leaping from the armchair to confront him. Christobel Ross said quietly, 'I was at home with my daughter. We were having our evening meal together. To save you from further enquiry, I must tell you that there were no adult witnesses to my presence there, and that I do not wish you to question a child of five about whether her mother might be lying.'

Holmes nodded. 'Very well. There is one further enquiry I must make, however. As an army officer, your late husband would have been issued with a pistol. Was the weapon returned to the military arsenal after his death?'

She turned for the first time to face him, weighing up the languid pose, the deep-set, watchful eyes in the long face. 'You are more direct than your friend, I see, Mr Holmes. And I begin to perceive how you have acquired your reputation for going to the heart of the matter. No, the pistol was not returned to the military. I found it in its holster, at the bottom of the box of effects which was shipped home from India after Robert's death. I suppose with a death from typhus they were only too anxious to be rid of everything the victim had handled. I knew I should have handed the pistol in, but I did not know where to take it. And I suppose I had an obscure feeling that one day I might need it.'

She stared Holmes steadily in the face on that thought.

SIX

I had rarely seen Holmes eat so hearty a breakfast as he did on the morning after our investigation of the shooting at Blackheath Golf Club. He even congratulated Mrs Hudson on the excellence of her bacon and the consistency of her kedgeree – a rare compliment from a man who often seemed scarcely to notice what he was eating.

He waited until I had finished. Then he lit his briar, stretched his long legs in front of the fire and puffed smoke contentedly at the ceiling. I could not escape the feeling that I was delivering lines he had been waiting for as I said, 'You seem remarkably equable today, Holmes. Do you not fear an escalation of the violent events at Blackheath?'

'Oh, I don't think so, Watson. I shall be surprised if there is more shooting there before the end of the spring. But you obviously do not agree with me.'

'I think you are remarkably sanguine if you really believe that. I should be amazed if the man who is the victim of this violence is as calm about it as you are.'

'Alfred Bullimore? Well. I suppose you may be right. In which case, it is good that you will be able to test your theory in about an hour's time. The victim of the mysterious atrocity of Wednesday night should be with us by ten-thirty this morning.'

'You have asked him to come to Baker Street? Then you obviously think he is safer away from Blackheath at the moment.'

Holmes pursed his lips, weighing the thought. 'A possible deduction. But not the only one, and in this case the wrong one.'

'Then please stop looking so smug and tell me what is the right one!'

'It is simple enough, my old friend. I anticipated that you would wish to analyse the results of yesterday's enquiries with me. I have no objection to that: on the contrary, I find it a useful exercise in clarifying my own thoughts and ensuring that I have not overlooked any important factors. In this case, I thought it would be useful to have the central figure in this business present to hear our deliberations, and perhaps contribute his own thoughts upon the various parties involved. Before we left Blackheath last night, I invited Mr Bullimore to join us at ten-thirty this morning. He accepted the invitation, not perhaps with alacrity, but with a certain amount of enthusiasm.'

'No doubt with as much enthusiasm as anyone could expect, when his own life was at the centre of the discussion,' I said drily.

Bullimore came swiftly up the stairs to our rooms in his now familiar brown tweeds, ruddy of countenance, exuding an air of boisterous health that seemed quite inappropriate in someone who had so narrowly and so recently escaped death.

I greeted him and said I trusted the injury to his arm was healing well. He said it was, and was looking rather shame-faced when Holmes said jovially, 'It is healing quite exceptionally well, I think, Watson. For it appears our friend has been out on the links this very morning.'

'I have indeed. But how on earth –?'

'The blade of bent grass which has lodged in the folds of your jacket, Mr Bullimore,' said Holmes affably, deftly retrieving an inch-long fragment of grass from a fold near the side pocket of the Secretary's jacket. He held it up to the light. 'Not the type of grass to be found in a lawn, such as those well-tended areas you enjoy round your clubhouse, but common on the heathland terrain which characterises the wilder parts of your course. Dislodged, I fancy, by one of your more vigorous strokes from the rough.'

Bullimore smiled at me ruefully. 'I confess it, Dr Watson: indeed, there seems no point in trying to disguise anything from this observant friend of yours. I played nine holes this morning before I came here. A little tentatively at first – hence my excursion into the rough on the second, from which this evidence no doubt derived. But with increasing vigour, for the arm, although a little sore, stood up well to the test. I believe I shall be able to play eighteen tomorrow!'

He stood with feet apart in the middle of the room, beaming like a small boy trying unsuccessfully to look modest in the light of some startling achievement. I began to remonstrate with him about the folly of his actions, but saw from his face that my counsel would be useless. I contented myself with a little advice about the necessity of keeping wounds clean as they healed.

'I shall do that, of course, but I cannot get over my good fortune in getting away so lightly. And there is no time to lose! The season begins in earnest next week with a tournament in the West Country, and I plan to play tournaments in most of the weeks to come as part of my preparation for the Open championship at Muirfield.'

'I am gratified to hear it. It will at any rate remove you from Blackheath and your would-be assassin. Are the members resigned to losing their Secretary for such a long period?'

'Those were the conditions upon which I accepted the post. I shall be back for most of the weekends, and in any case most of the chaps are happy to see a Blackheath man figuring in the big tournaments alongside the professionals. I expect you know of John Ball and Harold Hilton, both amateurs who've won the Open championship against all comers in the 'nineties. Perhaps I shall become the third man to do it. I certainly won't fail for lack of effort!'

His blue eyes shone with enthusiasm, and I was struck again by the degree to which a man's whole life could be dominated by a game. Perhaps Holmes had the same feeling, for he now said abruptly, 'Let us therefore report without delay on our findings at Blackheath yesterday.'

I said, a little pompously I fear, 'We shall relay to you our findings, Alfred, and listen with interest to your comments upon them. Let us begin with your greenkeeper, Bevan.'

'Sound man, Bevan. I'm sure he had nothing to do with this.'

'Even though he has a strong reason to dislike you?'

Bullimore reddened: he had clearly not expected such directness from me. 'He told you I was planning to replace him? Well, it was nothing personal, you know. I simply thought that the best interests of the club might be served by –'

'Bevan didn't tell us, no. We found out the situation elsewhere in the club.'

'I see. Well, we discussed it at the meeting of the Committee, so I suppose there are a few people who know about it. I'm glad Bevan didn't tell you himself. He's a good worker and it shows he's not a troublemaker.'

'Does it? I thought on the contrary that it might implicate him in this affair. He concealed the fact that he had a motive to be rid of you. Could he hope to retain his job if you were out of the way?'

Bullimore frowned. 'I see what you mean. I suppose he might hope to remain head man, under another secretary. Not all the Committee were happy with my plan to replace him with a younger man. They felt he'd been a good servant over the years. Perhaps they had a point; when I consider the matter now, I think I was perhaps a little hasty myself, in expecting him to work on at reduced wages under another man.'

Bullimore looked as if he was considering the effect on the man's feelings for the first time, and it is possible that it was so. He seemed, as several of the members at Blackheath had pointed out to us, curiously insensitive about the effects of his words and actions upon others. I said, 'It's the kind of proposal that would make a man bitter, when he knows he's been a conscientious worker. Has it occurred to you that Bevan's presence in his hut meant that he was the man nearest to the scene of the ambush?'

'Well, yes. For one thing, he was the first person on the scene to help me.'

'Yes, after an interval of a few seconds. He could easily have fired the pistol, disappeared into the bushes, and re-emerged as though he had come from his greenkeeper's shed.'

'I suppose so.'

'Bevan claims that he heard no sound of anyone making off after the shot. That is surely hardly likely, in view of his proximity.'

'Perhaps not. But my attacker was moving over soft ground, and may not have gone directly past his hut.'

I thought of the absence of foot marks and of my conclusion that the gunman was lightly built, possibly even female. It was Holmes who said, 'Indeed, your attacker might have disappeared in the opposite direction entirely. In other words, he might have gone back into the golf club whence he came, Mr Bullimore.'

I had seen that narrowing of my friend's grey eyes too often before not to realise that this was a key moment, that Holmes was studying the central figure in all this for some reaction which might indicate a suspicion of a particular member of staff, or perhaps a member of the golf club. Perhaps Bullimore too was conscious of the importance of the moment. He was sitting now, but he did not look at either of us as he said slowly, 'That is possible; of course it is. I have to accept that this is someone who knows all about my movements. But if it is someone who works at the golf club, or even one of the members, I have no idea who it might be.'

'Then we must see if the conversations we conducted yesterday suggest further thoughts to you,' said Holmes briskly. 'Tell us what your notes on Marcel Lebrun contain, Watson.'

'Not a lot. But we must bear in mind that he fulfils the

conditions for a suspect which the previous incidents demand: he has a good knowledge of your movements and he
is in the club for long hours every day. He also had ample
opportunity: he claims that he was in the kitchen alone at
the time of the attack on you, but we found no one to
corroborate that fact. He could easily have slipped out and
been waiting for you in the bushes.'

Bullimore nodded slowly, weighing the idea. Holmes
said, 'How much do you know about Lebrun, Mr Bullimore?'

'Very little. He's a good chef, or he wouldn't have kept
his job at the club. He has a rough manner and he can be
surly, even temperamental. But he doesn't come into contact with the members much; as long as his food is good,
his manner scarcely matters.'

I said gently, 'He does not seem to like you much, this
Marcel Lebrun. Can you think of any reason for that?' I
was thinking of the chef shrugging his huge, expressive
shoulders and saying that he did not like the way the
Secretary treated women, but I could not relay that reaction
directly to Bullimore. It would not be fair on the chef to
repeat his private thoughts to the man who employed him.

Bullimore said, 'No. It is not always possible to be both
efficient and popular with the people who work for you.'

I was sure that he was holding something back from us
here; in the light of what Mrs Ross had told us, I wondered
if Gallic chivalry had provoked some outburst from the
chef on her behalf. But all I said was, 'I understand he has
rooms which look out over the golf course. He is in a good
position to observe your movements, to know when you are
in and out of the clubhouse.'

Bullimore smiled. 'If you mean to imply that I spend a

good deal of my time out on the course, you are quite right. I work hard to improve my game, as you know, and I make no apology for that. Those are the terms on which I took on the job of Secretary.'

'I intended no slur, Alfred. I merely remind you that Lebrun, who works different hours from you, is able to observe your movements outside the clubhouse as well as in it. He would know when was the best time to slip the letters which began all this into your office without detection, for instance. He would know that you play alone on the course in the early part of the day, and he could have left the note in the shelter on the course which brought you here on that first day almost three weeks ago.'

'That is true. And Lebrun, though a good chef, came without a reference from his last employer in France. We took him on for a trial fortnight originally. He is clearly a volatile man, and I'm fairly sure he has been involved in violence at some time, but I can give you no details.'

I looked at Holmes, repressing a smile; he had accused me of prejudice against foreigners when I had voiced my doubts about this man. My companion said sardonically, 'Dr Watson, as an enlightened professional man, thinks that this man's limited English and large black moustache make him a leading suspect. Have you ever seen Lebrun with a firearm?'

'Never. But of course I have never had occasion to search his rooms or inspect his belongings.'

'Quite. Well now, what about your fellow-members, Mr Bullimore? We can rule out no one on occasions like this, as I'm sure you realise by now.'

The Secretary shook his head in bafflement. 'I do see

that. I've forced myself to consider that this might be one of the members. They are a varied lot, as you might expect, but for the life of me I cannot see any of them being involved in this.'

'"For the life of you" might be a frighteningly accurate phrase,' said Holmes acidly. 'Let us therefore put some of the possibilities before you. Shall we start with Herbert Robinson?'

Bullimore was plainly surprised, but he did not rule the idea out of court altogether. 'He's around the club more than most, certainly. More than anyone, in fact, I should think. And I know he doesn't like me much – I think he thinks I spend too much time on the course and playing in the big tournaments. But as I said, those were the terms on which I took the job, and he knows it.'

Robinson had also said that the Secretary wasn't very sensitive to the thoughts and needs of others, but Bullimore did not mention this. I doubt if he was even conscious of it, or even of the need for a Secretary to consider such things. He was so devilishly bound up with himself and his own progress in golf that I was sure by now that he didn't even consider the social aspects of his post at all important. I said, 'I agree, having talked to him, that it is difficult to see Herbert Robinson taking a gun to you.'

Bullimore laughed, that abrupt and sudden sound which I had heard burst from him a couple of times when we had played on the course together. 'Scarcely! He is built for comfort rather than speed, old Herbert. I can't quite see him making off rapidly through the bushes!'

I was a little piqued by his contemptuous dismissal of an enemy on physical grounds, perhaps because I could imagine him dismissing my golf in the same way. I said irritably, 'You can't rule him out on those grounds! A man like Robinson would employ some villain to do the dangerous work, not stand in the cold and the twilight to wait for you himself.'

'I suppose you're right. But I can't see old Herbert feeling strongly enough about me to want me removed from this earth, all the same!'

Holmes intervened. 'Nor can I, Mr Bullimore, nor anyone else, I fancy. But I said to Watson at the outset of this case that there is madness in it somewhere. And madness, as you will be aware, sometimes manifests itself in the least predictable quarter.'

Bullimore's blue eyes turned their bright gaze upon Holmes. 'I had not considered the possibility of madness. Yet it is logical to do so, as you say – indeed, it is the only explanation which makes any sense. But it would surely mean that the net must be cast very wide, since madness, as you say, can lurk in the most unexpected places.' His weatherbeaten features shone with a new animation, as if excited by a whole new range of thoughts.

'Indeed, though that is scarcely a consoling thought, when we have your safety to consider. If you do not think Herbert Robinson is a candidate for murder, then what of Edward Frobisher?'

Bullimore smiled, then held up his powerful hand. 'Forgive me if I seem frivolous. The thought of Edward Frobisher beset by madness affords a certain uncharitable amusement, since he presents himself always as the sanest and most practical of men. Yes, I suppose he is a candidate. Beneath his urbane and cultivated exterior, he could be a dangerous enemy. For an enemy he is, I have no doubt of that. He expected to be made Secretary when I took the job, and it was easy to see that my appointment was a real blow to him. Indeed, he made no secret of the fact that he thought he should have had the job. I think he still feels that, but I thought he had got over the worst of his resentment. We rub along together in a sort of civilised neutrality, not speaking very much in the clubhouse, but conducting ourselves quite properly in meetings, even when we disagree.'

'Could he have been in those bushes behind the clubhouse on Wednesday night?'

Bullimore was serious enough now. His face was full of intelligent consideration as he said, 'He could, certainly. He was in the group who gathered round me when Bevan helped me into the clubhouse and my arm was bleeding so freely. It was Frobisher who sent for the doctor, I think. And he could certainly have arranged for some villain to fire the pistol on his behalf. He's a lawyer, with a flourishing practice, though he isn't much involved himself any more. But they must be in contact with criminals enough, mustn't they, lawyers?'

Holmes smiled. 'They are in a position to run the underworld of London, if only they had the will. Fortunately most of them don't. But do not rush away to Blackheath to confront Frobisher, please. We shall register him as a possibility for your assailant, no more.'

We discussed one or two other members whose names Bullimore gave us, then moved on to the employees of the golf club. I was particularly interested in the caddies, who emerged as a dubious lot. Bullimore had already asked the caddiemaster to check on their whereabouts at the time of the attack – a considerable task, as most of them were part-time employees and many of them had not even volunteered a fixed address to the man who directed them. The difficulty was that since Alfred Bullimore invariably carried his own clubs, he did not have a close acquaintance with any of them. Beyond a certain resentment that he chose not to employ them, none seemed to have any particular reason to hate him. The most one could say was that many of them were perennially short of money and that several of them had previous instances of violence in their backgrounds, though much of this was in domestic disputes or tavern brawls. I pointed out, and my companions readily agreed, that their numbers might well provide a man desperate enough to take on a shooting on someone else's account.

Holmes allowed so much to this view as to add, 'It would account for the inaccuracy of this shooting, certainly. It might take a man unfamiliar with firearms to miss from such close range.'

'Or a woman, of course,' I said quietly, emboldened by his support.

Bullimore started violently. There was only one woman it might have been, I supposed. In 1896, it was not thought seemly for women to arch their bodies into golf swings, and Blackheath had no lady members. There were maids and cleaning women enough about the place, but none of these was likely to have much direct contact with the Secretary.

Bullimore read my mind easily enough, though clearly he thought me impertinent. 'If you mean Mrs Ross, then –'

'We do,' said Holmes shortly.

'And we know that you once cared deeply for the lady,' I added quickly. I did not want him going into long protestations of the distance between them: that could only have led to more embarrassment on both sides.

There was a long moment's silence, during which the Secretary's heavy breathing was the only sound in the room, and the noise of the cart wheels on the cobbles outside rang unnaturally loud in our ears. Then, with a composure which must have cost him much effort, he said, 'And who told you of what has been between us? Was it Christobel Ross herself?'

Holmes, who had much experience of such questions, said dismissively, 'The source of our information is of no matter now, Mr Bullimore. You might like to know that our initial information did not come from the lady herself. Perhaps, indeed, it would have been more appropriate if we had found out about the affair from you yourself. When I am asked to conduct an investigation, I expect to be furnished with all the known facts about it at the outset.'

I thought for a moment that Bullimore was going to bridle at the rebuke. His face made me think that I should not like to be an employee of Blackheath Golf Club unless I were confident of my skills. But all he eventually said was, 'I did not think it had any relevance to the thing I came to see you about. Mrs Ross had nothing to do with this, I'm sure.'

'You had much better let us be the judges of that, Mr Bullimore. Dr Watson has lots of theories about hell having no fury worse than a woman scorned, and I am bound to say that the history of crime gives him considerable support. And I am sure that most of the slain lovers thought as you do that the lady could intend no serious ill to them.'

Bullimore rubbed his knuckle through his dark moustache as he weighed this. 'I suppose you're right. Nevertheless, I must reiterate that I'm sure Christobel had nothing to do with this business – neither the letters nor the violence which has followed them.'

'That is good to hear. However, it won't prevent us testing her innocence for ourselves. How long is it since you enjoyed your close relationship with this lady?'

Bullimore looked at Holmes furiously for a moment, then said dully, 'It is about fifteen months, I think, since our relationship deepened. Christobel had been at Blackheath for about three months. She was – is – a very good worker, and I realised quickly that she would be a most efficient assistant for me on the three mornings when she was present. She is also, as you must have noticed, a very beautiful woman.'

'Oh, Dr Watson certainly noticed that, Mr Bullimore. In the most dispassionate way, of course,' smiled Holmes. 'Whereas you, presumably, reacted in a rather more positive way?'

Bullimore had flashed a look at me which had the vividness of jealousy. Now he turned his head furiously back to Holmes. 'Look here, I'm not here to defend myself about Christobel. I realise now that she was lonely, and I suppose you think I took advantage of that.'

'Whether you did or did not is not our concern, Mr Bullimore. We do not sit here in moral judgement: there are far too many people in London ready to do that without invitation. We wish to establish the facts of the case, so that we may decide how to proceed: the case which you have brought to us, remember.'

'All right! All right, I'll tell you all I can. Christobel was lonely, beautiful and working close to me on three mornings a week. I suppose if I am honest I was rather lonely too; I sowed my wild oats as a young man, but I hadn't had much female company in the nineties. Anyway, we became quite close fairly quickly.'

'Did you give Mrs Ross the idea that you were intending to marry her?'

'Look here Holmes, I —'

'It's necessary, I assure you. And there is no need to protect the privacy of the lady: she has already been very frank with us.'

'Very well.' Bullimore looked as if the lady's privacy was the last thing he had been thinking of. He was red with embarrassment, more discomfited than he had seemed even when his life had been in mortal danger. 'Christobel resisted my advances at first, but I could see she was keen. I don't remember what I might have said to get things moving.'

The picture of a man with blood pulsing and lust driving him forward might have been comic if the situation had been less serious. Holmes's expression did not alter. He said only, 'So Mrs Ross might have had the impression at least that you were planning marriage, and a new home for her daughter.'

'She might. All right, I know she did! Because that was the source of our eventual break-up.'

'You no longer intend to wed the lady?'

'No. I never did. She wanted marriage. Wanted a commitment I was not prepared to give to her, in the end. 'Oh,

I don't claim to have behaved very honourably, but you said you wanted the facts, didn't you?'

'Exactly. And the facts indicate an able and resourceful woman who feels that she has been deceived. A woman who has to go on working at close quarters with the man who she feels has wronged her. A woman who might now feel passionately resentful about that situation.'

'I suppose so. I know Christobel thinks I deceived her, and perhaps she's right. But I'm sure she wouldn't do anything to harm me.'

'Hmm. Did you know that Mrs Ross is still in possession of her husband's army pistol?'

Bullimore looked thoroughly shaken by that. 'No. Are you saying . . . ?'

'I'm saying nothing. It may or may not be significant that the lady had kept that information from you. Where was she at the time of the shooting on Wednesday night?'

'At home, I think. She certainly wouldn't be around the club at that time. She only works in the mornings.'

But Holmes and I knew, having questioned her, that she could not prove her whereabouts at the time of the ambush. I couldn't help thinking at that moment of the absence of heavy footprints around the scene of the shooting, of Holmes's guiding me to the thought that it might have been a woman who had stood there in the near-darkness of those bushes.

Holmes studied the Secretary in turmoil for a moment. Then he said crisply, 'Who do you think is trying to kill or injure you, Mr Bullimore?'

Bullimore was plainly taken aback by the directness of this. 'I – I don't know, do I?'

'On the contrary, you are the person best placed to make an intelligent deduction. We have already agreed that your opponent is almost certain to be someone known to you. You are the person who best understands the intricacies of your relationships with others. I am not asking you to provide us with the evidence the police would need for an arrest; I am merely asking you to name the person you think most likely to have perpetrated this series of acts against you.'

Bullimore thought for a moment, his healthy, outdoor face looking increasingly drawn. Then he said, 'No. I can't help you, I'm afraid.'

'Can't help yourself, you mean. That is a pity, but it does not altogether surprise me. What do you want us to do next?'

I felt it was time to intervene. 'Surely, Holmes, we must go back to Blackheath, mustn't we? We must investigate further the activities of the people of whom we have spoken today, and any others Alfred thinks may have had the wish and the opportunity to harm him.'

Holmes neither confirmed nor denied the view. Instead, he looked steadily at the third man in the room. 'Well, Mr Bullimore, does that seem a sensible strategy to you or not?'

The Secretary did not show the eagerness I should have expected from one in his perilous position. He hesitated a little, then said, 'I can't deny the logic of that, though I can see it might take up a lot of your time with little tangible result – this fellow has covered his tracks very effectively, I think. As I said, I am going to be away from the club myself for much of the spring and summer. It seems to me that as the hostility seems to centre entirely upon me, our criminal may well choose to lie low in my absence.'

'I agree with that,' said Holmes.

I tried to direct the discussion back to what we should do next, but Bullimore seemed relieved to move away from talk of any danger to his life. He enlarged upon the details of the golf tournaments he intended to play, listing the great men of the game who would be playing alongside him. As always when he spoke of golf, his face shone with a boyish enthusiasm, and his computation of the odds against his success drove out all other thoughts. I was struck, and indeed irritated, by the degree to which this game eliminated all other considerations, including that of his personal safety. The man, as Christobel Ross had told us so bitterly, was a fanatic. Golf left no room in his life for ordinary human considerations.

Perhaps he eventually detected a little of my disapproval. He said apologetically, 'Well, I must not take up any more of your time, gentlemen. Be assured that I shall think of you sometimes, when I am not involved in the golfing challenges which lie ahead. I am sure I shall be very much safer away from Blackheath and my mysterious enemy!'

It was a full month before the irony of those words became apparent.

SEVEN

I waited anxiously through the days which followed for news of further villainy at Blackheath. There was none. When the days lengthened into weeks and the weeks stretched towards a month, I became impatient for news. Holmes was away from Baker Street, busy with concerns which I may well report at some future date, for I have my notes of them. Eventually, I determined to find out for myself just what was going on out at that quiet golf club.

I confess I was slightly disappointed when I found that there appeared to be nothing at all. I took myself and my golf sticks out to the course and played there on a bright April day, when clouds raced fast across a bright blue sky and the larks sang clear and shrill, rising with spring exuberance until they were invisible above me. I was using my supposed interest in golf as a cover for my inquisitiveness, but in fact I found myself enjoying the exercise and the challenge of the ancient game in such exhilarating conditions.

My satisfaction may have had more than a little to do with the fact that on this visit I found myself an opponent much nearer to my own standard in the game than Alfred Bullimore had been on my previous venture on to the links. I played with Herbert Robinson, florid of complexion, strenuous of effort, and startlingly inventive in the language he bestowed upon his ball. I understood his feelings – my own tribulations ensured that I could not fail to do so – but I realised even more clearly why this was not considered a game for ladies.

Robinson was in better practice than me, but in much worse physical condition, though I have to admit that I had the advantage of some fifteen years over him. We each threw a hole or two at the other, but contested the rest in fairly even mediocrity, with the occasional stroke of startling brilliance enlivening the dross. It was a far cry from my game with Bullimore; I appreciated now what a thing of beauty his game was. I even understood a little of his passion for golf, when I executed a stroke which pleased me. I eventually won the game on the eighteenth, when Robinson conceded the hole after several shots in a bunker and a series of increasingly lurid linguistic outbursts.

We repaired to the bar, where Robinson confirmed that there had been no further outbreaks of violence around the club, and, as far as he knew, no further threats to its Secretary. 'Fellow is away from the club a damned sight too much, in my view!' he said grumpily. 'Still, at least he seems to have taken the horseplay away with him.'

This seemed scarcely fair to the Secretary, who was the innocent centre of this mysterious outbreak of villainy in the quiet suburb. But it was hardly the moment to challenge my portly companion, who was glaring into his whisky glass and meditating upon his defeat. I found that other members were altogether more favourably disposed towards Alfred Bullimore.

They were excited by the success he was enjoying against

the cream of the country's golfers in the spring tournaments. 'He even gave J.H. Taylor a run for his money on his own links, down at Westward Ho! in Devon,' said one in awed tones. There were cuttings from *The Morning Post* on the notice board in the hall, with Bullimore's scores underlined in red ink; he had figured prominently in the last two tournaments.

Most of the championships then were conducted on a match-play basis, and my friend – as I now felt privileged to call him – had acquitted himself well. He had won one of the smaller competitions in East Anglia, and subsequently reached two semi-finals and a final against excellent fields. I read that, as one of the men in prime form, he was fancied to do well in the following month's big event, at Sandwich in Kent, and there was even mention of him as an outsider for the Open championship itself at Muirfield.

And despite Robinson's surly attitude, the club did not seem to be suffering in his absence. I went into the office to see Mrs Ross, and found the lady thoroughly on top of the work there and looking very much better than when we had last seen her. She told me contentedly that there had been no repetition of the anonymous letters in Bullimore's absence, no further outbreaks of petty violence such as the one in which old Captain Osborne and his poor dog had suffered, and no threats to anyone else in the club. Moreover, Bullimore, who had come into the club in the intervals between tournaments, had been able to confirm that the violence had not pursued him to other parts of the country. 'He seemed almost to have forgotten about it,' she said, shaking her pretty head at the thought. 'He talked of nothing but his golf, as usual. I had almost to remind him that he had been in great physical danger.'

I could picture him as she said it, standing foursquare in his tweed jacket in this very room, describing his success elsewhere, able to entertain no thoughts but those of his own progress to the pinnacles of the game. I could not but feel compassion for this most beguiling creature with the soft grey eyes, who had been so sadly let down by him. 'It may be that you are well rid of him, my dear,' I said softly. 'I fear he is too single-minded a man to have made a good husband.'

She sighed. 'Single-minded to the point of obsession, Dr Watson. I wish I had realised that before I compromised myself. But I shall survive. I only hope that Alfred will.' She smiled a bitter smile on this dark thought, looking past me and out of the window.

I did not like the sound of that, but she would not elaborate upon it, so I left her as quickly as I could. I found no such reticence when I went for a few words with Marcel Lebrun, who was busy in his kitchen. He said the club was a happier place without its Secretary, then muttered darkly that a man who treated women as Bullimore did could expect to come to no good. I pressed him to tell me what he meant by this, but he gave me merely a shrug of his massive Gallic shoulders and a snort of impatience. Then he began to hammer the steak upon his chopping board with noisy vigour. I deduced that he had a soft spot for the fair Christobel Ross. I, of course, am proof against female charms, but she had certainly aroused sympathy in even as objective a breast as mine.

I had seen the head greenkeeper, Bevan, when we were on the course, but I now sought him out and found him in his shed, sharpening the very scythe which he claimed to have been honing at the time of the attack on Bullimore some fifteen yards away from this spot. Like the chef before him, he seemed more cheerful and confident with the Secretary away from the course and the clubhouse. Bevan thought the plan to replace him with a younger man had now been dropped, and even seemed to entertain some vague notion that he had Holmes and me to thank for the change.

I went so far as to reveal my deduction from the absence of deep heel-marks in the place where the attacker had stood that it was probably a woman or a slightly built man who had held the gun to shoot down Bullimore. Bevan seemed excited by the idea, and I thought for a moment it had suggested to him who that mysterious ambusher had been, but if he had any candidate for the outrage, he elected not to reveal the name to me. He had two boys of fourteen and fifteen helping him on the course and learning the trade; I registered the fact to report to Holmes before I moved on.

The caddiemaster had been vetting the men who carried bags around the course. They were a motley crew, in temperament and background as well as dress, but he was fairly satisfied that none of his regular men had been involved in the violence against the Secretary. Many of them had regular clients among the members, who were prepared to speak for their honesty and reliability. He was not so sure about the men who carried bags on a casual and haphazard basis; they turned up mostly at the weekends, when the course was busier, and picked up whatever bag they could get. Many of these men disappeared for weeks at a time, and he was sure a few of them had done time in prison. The caddiemaster had unearthed no one with a personal grievance against Bullimore, but it was certainly possible that there lurked among the caddies men who would be desperate enough to wound and even kill for the right sum of money.

The last person I saw before I left was Edward Frobisher. He was more friendly and open than during our previous meetings. He said that, though as a lawyer he was naturally cautious, he was hopeful that the trouble which had beset the club and centred on its Secretary was now at an end. The villainy did not seem to have pursued Bullimore on his travels around the country; hopefully it would not surface again when he returned to Blackheath. Alfred was not a bad fellow after all, he said cheerfully, and the excellence of his golf on some of the best links in England was helping to put the club on the map.

This was a great shift from the recriminations he had given us previously, when his disappointment that Bullimore had been preferred to him for the Secretary's post had seemed to colour his whole attitude. I looked forward to discussing the significance of the change with Holmes. Frobisher said as he rose that he hoped that I would come to play at the club again, and we ended by arranging to play together in three weeks' time. 'I shall hope to give you a better challenge than Herbert managed!' he said jovially as I prepared to leave. I said I looked forward to it, as indeed I did, having rekindled my enthusiasm for this most frustrating of games. I also harboured hopes of finding out rather more from the shrewd and suddenly more responsive Edward Frobisher.

Alas, our contest never took place! It was forestalled by events of an altogether more dramatic nature. I began to follow Alfred Bullimore's progress avidly in the national prints, enjoying some of the vicarious satisfaction one always does when a friend or acquaintance acquits himself well at the highest level. My man pulled off a victory against a small but select field in Sussex. Then, two weeks later, he was in a field of sixty-four in the match-play event at Sandwich in Kent, which everyone said was the last serious tournament before the Open championship in Scotland.

He won his first round easily, then defeated one of the favourites at the first extra hole after what *The Times* described as a 'pulsating struggle'. According to their correspondent, there was every prospect that 'the strong and confident figure of Alfred Bullimore could stride all the way to the final', though the writer could not see him triumphing there against the formidable professional George Jackson, who was moving easily through the other half of the draw.

Holmes had returned briefly to Baker Street, listened quietly but without his usual incisive questioning to my account of my latest expedition to Blackheath, and then travelled away again to Westmoreland. I determined that if Bullimore survived until the final, I would take the train down to Sandwich at the end of the week and see how he got on against this fellow Jackson. Alfred was going from strength to strength: I was not as sure as the eminent correspondent of *The Times* that the great professional would have the easy victory he seemed to expect.

My plans were harshly disrupted on the evening before I planned to travel to Sandwich. I caught the name of the town through the news-seller's almost incomprehensible cries. I stopped dead in the street when I read the headline in *The Star*.

GOLFER SHOT DURING PLAY AT SANDWICH

My first thought was that poor Alfred had been killed. His enemy must have followed him, bided his time, caught him off guard when he was concerned with nothing but his golf. But when I read the hastily assembled columns beneath the headline, I realised with relief that Alfred was safe.

The man who had been shot was the most famous golfer in the competition, the great George Jackson himself.

EIGHT

I packed a suitcase quickly and prepared to catch a train to Sandwich that very night. Neither I nor Mrs Hudson were certain of exactly where Holmes was, so I could not dispatch a telegram to him with the news of what had happened in Kent. I knew that if he were near to the climax of a case in the north, his single-mindedness in pursuit of a solution would mean he had no time for newspapers. I should have to use my own initiative to follow up the violence which had disrupted the golf tournament on the south coast; I confess that I relished the prospect of showing my old friend how much I had learned from him.

I had no means of knowing where Alfred Bullimore was staying in the town. I had to change on to a slow local train in Canterbury, so that it was far too late when I arrived in Sandwich to try to seek him out that night. But I knew where I would find my friend on the morrow. Indeed, I had dispatched a telegram to him care of the St George's Club, Sandwich, where the golf tournament was taking place, confident that he would be one of the first people there in the morning.

Had I been visiting Sandwich in less sinister circumstances, I should have thoroughly enjoyed the experience. I had taken the first hotel room I could secure, relying on the advice of the cab driver I had picked up at the station. He had not let me down. The room, like the hotel, was unpretentious but clean, and although I had ordered breakfast at seven, the food was wholesome and beautifully presented on Royal Worcester plates. I had the dining-room to myself at that hour; I looked out over green slopes to a sky and a sea of as sharp and deep a blue as anything in the Mediterranean.

The hotel had a pleasant elevation in the old town, which is some little distance from the ocean. The golf course was between me and the sea, an exhilarating links of the traditional sort. As I walked down to it, the crisp, clear air had a bite which reminded me that winter was still not too far behind us, but by the time I reached the clubhouse, the larks were trilling in the clear air above the course, as if in celebration of this glorious day and the summer still to come.

I found Alfred Bullimore easily enough, as I had suspected I might; indeed I recognised him from some distance away. A distinctive, sturdy figure, in the russet tweeds I had come to see as characteristic of him, he was hitting practice balls on the area behind the clubhouse which had been set aside for the purpose. Even in the face of this latest outrage, even after the bizarre eruption of violence in this peaceful setting, Alfred was not to be diverted from his golf and his pursuit of the pinnacles of the game. He was studying the flight of the balls he struck away so effortlessly as keenly as if he had been back at Blackheath before this awful campaign against him began. I admired his dedication and self-possession, but I could not but fear his courage might be misplaced. There was madness in this business somewhere: even Sherlock Holmes had agreed with that view.

Bullimore was so immersed in his practice that he did not notice my arrival. I stood behind him for three or four minutes, listening to his steady breathing, admiring his technique as the balls accumulated in a small area a hundred and fifty yards away from us. Despite my irritation with the man's obsession with this game, I could not but marvel at the purity and accuracy of his striking with the mashie he swung so naturally.

Even when he finally noticed me, he did not desist from his practice. 'Be with you in a moment, John,' he said, his breathing scarcely uneven after fifty strokes. 'Just want to try flighting a couple lower; you need that shot here when the wind comes in off the sea.' He moved the next balls back a little in his stance, swinging the hickory shaft of the club more flatly, punching them away with an abbreviated follow-through. Sure enough, the balls flew lower through the breeze, running on over the close-cropped seaside turf when they pitched. It was a standard of expertise far beyond anything I could envisage for my own game. It showed a disregard for the events around him which I found positively annoying.

'We need to talk, Alfred,' I said abruptly, cutting out the niceties of greeting.

He nodded, gathering together the clubs which lay on the ground beside him. 'We still have forty minutes before I am due to play my semi-final,' he said calmly. His manner reminded me of some consultants I had known in my own profession, who granted an audience as though it were a favour which should never be taken for granted.

'The competition is going ahead?' I said incredulously.

'Oh, yes. We've had a meeting at the club about it this morning. One or two people were a little reluctant, in view of the injury to Jackson, but we know now that it isn't fatal, and I thought it much the best policy to press on. Mustn't let our anonymous gunman think he's caused us to abandon our tournament, or the bounder will think he's won, won't he?'

There was a certain brave logic in this, but also a disregard of the physical danger that threatened him, which seemed to me to be reckless rather than courageous. I said tersely, 'This creature is much more than a bounder, Alfred, and you must treat him accordingly. Where are the police?' I asked, thinking that I might need official support if I was to forestall this rash nonsense.

Bullimore looked round him, examining the clubhouse and its outbuildings, as if registering for the first time the thought that there might have been police activity here. 'The police are in the town, I expect,' he said. 'I told them all that I was able to last night. Hasn't Mr Holmes come with you?'

This seemed to show little gratitude for the way I had left my own business in London to dash to the man's help last night. 'He is busy with other concerns in the Northwest of England,' I said, placing my friend as far away geographically as I could, 'and I hope he is dealing there with clients who have a greater regard for their own safety than some people who have asked him for his help.'

Bullimore smiled. 'I have a prospect of winning a major tournament – especially now that poor Jackson has been so abruptly removed from contention. I cannot afford to neglect that opportunity.' His eyes looked past me to the deserted course; his lips set in that schoolboy determination to cut out all other concerns which I had sometimes seen in him before.

'You had better tell me exactly what happened yesterday,' I said heavily. 'I have seen only the briefest details in the stop press of *The Star*.'

'The shooting? Well, it didn't happen at the golf course.' He sounded like a cleric relieved that some outrage had at least not been perpetrated within the walls of his church. 'Jackson was shot on his way home from the club, last night, after he'd won his way through into the semi-final. He won quite easily, you know, five and four. He was much the best golfer in the field, and I was quite looking forward to –'

'Then this shooting might be an isolated incident, totally unrelated to the violence which has previously been offered to you? This might in fact be an attack on George Jackson? It might be armed robbery, or even someone with a personal grudge against Jackson?'

For a moment, a sly look stole across the normally open countenance of my infuriating friend. 'The police certainly think so. They are enquiring among the known criminals of the town.'

'But you don't think they will find the culprit there.'

'No, frankly I do not. Look here, Watson, the police know nothing of the events at Blackheath, as we agreed they shouldn't, and I'd like to keep it that way.'

'I don't think we can do that, now, Alfred. As you know, I didn't like the fact that we hadn't brought them into this at the time of the attack on you at Blackheath. I like it even less now.'

Again I saw that stubborn setting of the broad lips into a thinner line. 'I promised my members at Blackheath that we wouldn't sensationalise this. I think the police will stir up a hornets' nest, with very little prospect of finding the perpetrator of the attacks on me. That is why I came to Sherlock Holmes in the first place. It is a pity he cannot be here now.'

I felt my annoyance rising. 'Well, at any rate, I am here!' I snapped. 'You had better tell me exactly what happened. Is Jackson badly hurt?'

'I believe not. I have not seen him since the shooting, of course, but I am told his injuries are not life-threatening. He was shot from behind, which reinforces the view that someone followed him from here. Apparently two shots were fired, one of which hit him in the right thigh, just above the knee. It is still early days, but the surgeons have apparently said the damage is not irreparable. But they do not think he will be able to play again this season, poor fellow.'

It was characteristic of him that he should express the injuries in terms of golf. I said acidly, 'And what do *you* think, Alfred? Do you think the attack was entirely uncon-nected with previous events at Blackheath?'

We were now sitting on a bench beside the clubhouse, looking out towards the sea and the white horses which danced in the sun upon it. Bullimore paused for a long moment and checked that no one was within earshot before he said softly, 'No. I believe that last night's attack came from one and the same person. I believe that the bullet which felled George Jackson was intended for me.'

It was quietly spoken, but it carried utter conviction. I

was filled with a reluctant admiration for the mistaken, pig-headed courage of the man, who believed this, and yet wanted to go forward uninterrupted to whatever golfing triumphs awaited him. A small paddle-steamer was moving across the bay towards Ramsgate. We watched the long trail of smoke stretching out in the breeze behind it, each busy with our own thoughts. Eventually I said, 'What makes you so sure that the bullets were intended for you? Were you with George Jackson at the time?'

'No. I was a long way away from him. He is staying in a boarding house very near here. My hotel is in the old town, a mile and more away.'

'The paragraph in the stop press of *The Star* gave the impression that the shooting had happened on the golf course. I hadn't realised until now that it hadn't.' That explained why there had not been policemen swarming round the St George's Golf Club when I had arrived there, as I had expected.

'No. Jackson had an easy victory, as I told you. I was playing in the match behind him, but I finished almost an hour later. I won an exciting match on the last hole.' For a moment, I thought he was going to digress into the details of his hard-won victory. Perhaps my face warned him against it, for he went on, 'George is a professional, of course, and so not allowed into the members' section of the club, but he and a couple of his friends were having a drink with the club professional in his shop when I left the club and went back to my hotel.'

'What time was this?'

'About six o'clock.'

'And when did Jackson leave?'

'Well, of course, I couldn't be sure. But it was well after me; I must have been preparing for dinner in my hotel at the time. But I understand from the police that he was shot at about quarter to eight, whilst making the short journey back from here to the boarding house where he was staying.'

'Did he see anything of his attacker?'

'Nothing at all, according to the police. It was totally unexpected, of course, and he – well, he had been relaxing after his win for about three hours by then.'

'You mean he was drunk.'

'No! I mean he had been drinking, not that he was drunk. I do not believe that anyone who plays the game as well and as consistently as George Jackson makes a habit of getting drunk during a tournament.'

Again that respect for the game which bordered on fanaticism. It might in this case have been coming between Bullimore and his judgement. I said sternly, 'You mean you are not certain what condition Jackson was in when he was shot down. Well, I dare say the police will give me an opinion about that, when they hear that Sherlock Holmes has an interest in the case.'

Bullimore said stubbornly, 'I repeat that I would prefer that you made no connections with any previous violence at Blackheath. That could only lead to embarrassing questions as to why we did not inform them of those happenings earlier.'

'That is probably true. But I would remind you that it was my view that we should have informed the police of the series of events at Blackheath at the time when you were shot there.'

'But that was not my view. Nor was it that of Sherlock Holmes.'

'All right. I accept that. You may both have been wrong, that's all. What makes you think that last night's bullets were really intended for you?'

He glanced sideways at me, then looked out to sea again whilst he spoke. 'John, you saw me today long before I saw you. Indeed, when you spoke to me twenty minutes ago, I suspect you had located me, approached near to me, and stood watching me practice for some minutes before you spoke and I became aware of you.'

'Yes. That is certainly so. I recognised you from a hundred yards and more away as I came into the club.'

'Yes. And how would you say you first became aware that it was me?'

I wondered wryly who it was who was supposed to be doing the detective work here, but I indulged him. 'I know your habits well enough by now, Alfred. You have a massive, sometimes I think almost an unhealthy, devotion to the game of golf. I expected to find you hitting practice golf shots. You were exactly where I expected you to be, doing exactly what I expected you to be doing.'

He smiled, seeming to find my comments on his fanatical approach to the game rather a compliment than otherwise. 'But there were other people around – even, had you cared to notice them, one or two others practising. Yet you picked me out immediately from well over a hundred yards.'

'I expect you would like me to say that I identified you from the grace and rhythm of your golf swing, which I agree is distinctive. But the truth, I fear Alfred, is more mundane. I recognised your tweed golf outfit. You have played in similar garb every time I have seen you. I suppose for me it is the equivalent of one of these new-fangled trade marks which manufacturers are now using to identify their products.'

'Right! I thought as much. And you are right, of course: I have three very similar outfits, all in the same Harris Tweed. But let me now tell you that this week I have not worn this outfit until today. I was wearing jacket and trousers of a rather distinctive light green tweed. I had them made up some time ago, but found them a little garish, especially for the winter months at Blackheath. This week, in the bright, strong light of the seaside, I thought they would be less eye-catching.'

'I see. But what is the significance of this in the context of the attack on George Jackson?'

'The significance, Watson, is that Jackson was wearing exactly the same light green tweed as I was yesterday. I was playing behind him, and I remarked upon it myself. It is not a common shade. I fancy we are the only ones who have worn it this week.'

I saw now the drift of his reasoning. 'You believe that the attack upon Jackson was intended for you?'

He nodded. 'I am certain of it. I believe whoever was responsible waited for me to leave the club so as to shoot at me. As it happened, I was given a lift back to my hotel in a closed brougham by a spectator who had come down for the day from London. In the darkness, the attacker identified the wrong victim. He found poor Jackson reeling home a little uncertainly and took his chance to shoot at him and make off.'

It made sense, especially when he took me into the

changing-rooms and showed me the jacket of the tweed suit he had worn on the previous day. It was a rather lurid light green, of good quality, but not quite the hue I should have expected my friend to wear; Alfred had a conventional enough taste in clothes. I could see why he had waited for the bright artist's light of the seaside to mitigate the garish impact of this particular cloth.

It was now within twelve minutes of the starting time for Alfred's semi-final match, and I could see him becoming more impatient with each second. I got him to give me directions to the place where the attack on Jackson had taken place before he hurried away to the tee.

There was little to be learned there, save that this was an excellent place to waylay an unsuspecting victim. Jackson had been shot in an alley behind the row of terraced houses where he was lodging for the duration of the tournament at Sandwich. They were narrow, high houses, with small yards or gardens at the rear and wooden doors in a high brick wall which opened on to this cobbled rear access. The alley was unlit, and no doubt unfrequented at the time when Jackson had made his way home in the first hour of darkness. There were no signs of foot-marks on these dry cobbles, no method of ascertaining whether this gunman, like the one at Blackheath, had been of light enough build not to leave foot-marks in soft ground.

I had seen Holmes spend twenty minutes on hands and knees at the scene of a crime, but there was little here which could have warranted his intense scrutiny. I wandered up and down the alley for a while, and even found a dark stain which I was sure was the blood shed by George Jackson when he had fallen after the attack; it was within three yards of the rear door of the house where he was staying. But this merely confirmed the point of the attack, which I already knew. I wandered up and down the alley disconsolately in search of something more enlightening.

Then, just when I had decided that there was nothing useful here and I might as well go and see how my friend was faring in his semi-final match, I came upon a tiny piece of metal which set my pulses racing. It was at the far end of the alley, where a single scraggy hawthorn grew almost into the end of the crumbling brick wall. I wrapped my small trophy carefully in my handkerchief and prepared to take it back to Baker Street for Holmes to peruse.

The wall needed pointing. Nestling in its damaged mortar I had found a spent cartridge case, which I was sure was from the bullet which had narrowly missed George Jackson.

NINE

Alfred Bullimore won the tournament at Sandwich. I watched him come from two down in his semi-final to win two and one, after a fine niblick shot from a bunker on the seventeenth.

His opponent in the final was thoroughly rested, for he had enjoyed a walkover in the semi-final over the unfortunate George Jackson, who lay in the town hospital, but he seemed over-awed by his presence in a final he had never been expected to reach. Alfred, on the other hand, played like a man inspired, driving long and straight through what was now a brisk seaside breeze, playing his iron shots with an authority and confidence which surpassed even what I had by this time come to expect of him. He made a courteous winner's speech, complimenting the organisers and conveying everyone's sympathy and wishes for a speedy recovery to 'the finest golfer in the field', who had been so abruptly and brutally removed from their company.

The absence of George Jackson gave Bullimore's triumph a rather muted effect, but that was scarcely Alfred's fault. I talked to the police before I left Sandwich. I was fortunate that Inspector Forrest was in charge of the case, a man whom Holmes and I had met on a previous occasion, when Forrest had been grateful for the great man's help. He was immediately forthcoming about their enquiries in Sandwich. The police had turned up nothing among the local criminal fraternity, which by metropolitan standards was exceedingly small. 'Firearms are not the method of our local villains,' said Forrest. 'A heavy blow with a blackthorn cudgel or a shillelagh, yes, but rarely a firearm.'

'Was Jackson robbed?'

'It seems probably not. He is not a very good witness, since I fear he was half seas over at the time of the attack last night. He scarcely remembered walking home, let alone the details of the attack. He had only a few coins left in his pockets, but they appear to be untouched. And his watch, though only a cheap one, was still in the pocket of his jacket.'

'Did he see anything of his attacker?'

'Or attackers – we don't know how many were involved. No. If you ask me, it took him a minute or two to realise what had happened.'

'It might be worth your while to speak to him again, you know. I expect that apart from the drink, his brain would be affected by shock last night.'

Forrest nodded. 'We're going back to the hospital to see him again in the morning, Dr Watson. I don't expect him to recall anything that's useful about the attack, mind – don't forget he was shot from behind, in near-darkness. But he might be able to give us some idea of who perpetrated this – what enemies he's got, and which of them has access to a firearm and feels strongly enough to use it.'

'Ask him about these things by all means, Inspector. But I have another theory: I feel this may have been a case of mistaken identity.' I told him about the distinctive suits that Bullimore and Jackson had worn, which had set them apart visually from the rest of the field. And then, with some embarrassment, I told Forrest about the history of events at Blackheath, stretching now over three months and more since its petty commencement with the anonymous letters to the Secretary of the club.

He listened without comment but with increasing surprise to the story. 'And have none of these things been reported to the police, Dr Watson?'

'The attack on old Captain Osborne and his dog was investigated by the local constabulary. They discovered nothing useful.'

'But subsequent happenings have gone unreported, even when they culminated in shots being fired at the Secretary of the club?'

I was embarrassed, as I had known I would be. Mentally, I cursed Bullimore and Holmes for leaving me in this position. The one was too obsessed with his golf to have any proper perspective, I thought, and the other was becoming increasingly a law unto himself And here was I, a conventional, law-abiding citizen, who would have called the police in long ago, left to explain away their omissions. 'It was against my advice,' I said. 'Bullimore and his members had some idea of protecting the club from unwelcome publicity. Sherlock Holmes seemed to think he could solve the case without the help of police resources.'

'Well, he has done that often enough, I suppose,' said Forrest ruefully. 'But it seems that in this case at least, he was wrong. Can you get this chap Bullimore to report on his shooting, even at this late stage?'

'He doesn't want to involve the police. And as it happens,

he was very lucky – he was scarcely hurt at all. If it was the same man behind the pistol in both these cases, he wasn't much of a marksman – Bullimore didn't suffer much more than a graze and the attacker missed George Jackson with one bullet and hit him in the thigh with the other.'

'We don't know that he was shooting to kill, of course,' said Forrest. 'The evidence, such as it is, is rather to the contrary.'

My own thought was that this could have been the work of the most amateur of all marksmen: a woman who had never fired a pistol at all. I had an image in my mind of Mrs Christobel Ross, holding a smoking revolver in both hands, staring wide-eyed and open-mouthed at what she had done. But I kept the picture to myself. Forrest, who would not have been put in charge of any investigation at Blackheath himself, was swiftly persuaded that there was little point in pressing the matter, in the face of Bullimore's reluctance to co-operate. He said with a touching modesty, 'If Sherlock Holmes failed to find the culprit when the crime took place, there is very little chance of our turning up anything useful, at this distance in time. And if the victim is not prepared to co-operate, I think it would be very difficult for even Scotland Yard to mount a proper investigation.'

I promised him that if there was any further violence, or even any further threats delivered at Blackheath, I would take it upon myself to bring the police in immediately. For his part, he undertook to report any further useful evidence which he might turn up to 221B Baker Street.

Since Holmes was still not back, I ventured out to the old course at Blackheath again on the following Wednesday to play my delayed match with Edward Frobisher. We had a good tussle, which was much aided by the fact that I took a leaf out of Alfred Bullimore's book and practised my swing before we actually played our match.

I found the Blackheath rough much longer and more punishing now that we had moved into summer. Frobisher was lean and purposeful, with a very good grasp of the strengths and weaknesses of his own game. Unlike the portly Robinson, he did not take on shots that he did not think he could bring off. When he missed a green, he ran the ball in well whenever the opportunity offered, and threw very few shots away. The result was that he gave me four shots and still beat me on the eighteenth, though I played the best game I had so far managed over the taxing heathland course.

Edward Frobisher knew all about the events at Sandwich, since he and Herbert Robinson, along with two other members, had made the journey to watch their Secretary's performance in the most important tournament he had so far won. They had watched him win through to the semi-final on the very day when George Jackson had been shot, following him round the course during his wins in both morning and afternoon. I asked casually which train they had caught back to the capital, and made a mental note of the fact that it was the 8.13. Either Frobisher or Robinson, or for that matter either of the other two fellow-members who had journeyed to Sandwich with them, could have followed the figure in light green tweeds through the gathering darkness and shot him down. But would they, who knew the sturdy figure of Bullimore so well, have made the mistake of following Jackson? It was not impossible; indeed, I decided reluctantly that it was even probable, for there were no lights around the clubhouse at Sandwich, nor on the short route Jackson had taken to the alley where he had fallen.

Perhaps Frobisher saw the way my mind was working, for he gave me a grim smile. 'Any of us could have gone down there with the intention of damaging Bullimore, I know. And in case you're wondering, Thursday is Marcel Lebrun's day off duty – it is normally the quietest day in our dining-room. Bullimore himself has already pointed that out to me.'

'And did he say whether your greenkeeper, Bevan, was working on that Thursday?'

'No. But we give the head greenkeeper a fair amount of latitude in taking time off. He usually works at the week-ends and takes a day off whenever he thinks fit. Normally he tells the Secretary what day he will not be here, but of course Bullimore was down in Sandwich anyway. Do you want me to check now whether he was here on that Thursday?'

'No. I fancy there is no point in stirring up a hornets' nest. Anyone with a grievance against Bullimore could well have employed someone else to stand behind the gun. It would help to explain why whoever fired those bullets last Thursday night picked the wrong man. The real villain behind all this could have been walking about in Blackheath whilst the crime was being committed in Sandwich.'

I was persuaded as I spoke that this was the likeliest method, but it was a bleak prospect for those engaged in the detection of this crime, for the employment of an agent inevitably cast the field of suspects very wide. I kept my own counsel, but I was well aware that Mrs Ross also did not work on a Thursday, so that no one here could be aware of what she had been doing on the day when George Jackson had been shot.

Edward Frobisher and I had played at ten-thirty and followed our round with an excellent lunch: if Marcel Lebrun might possibly be a man with murder in his mind, he was nevertheless an excellent chef. In the middle of the afternoon, I left the lean, observant lawyer in the clubhouse and went to look for Alfred Bullimore. I knew by this time where I would find him when he was not in the clubhouse.

It was a blustery May day, with rain never far away and low cloud racing across a sullen sky. The weather had deteriorated since I had finished my game with Frobisher three hours earlier. There had already been a couple of showers; soon there would be more, no doubt, as the wind gusted in from the west over the nearby but invisible city of London. It was a pretty dismal scene. The golf course would have been deserted had it not been for the presence of one predictable figure.

Bullimore was hitting brassie and spoon shots up the fifth hole, rifling them long and low through the wind, getting them to bounce and run when they landed. He nodded a greeting, then went on hitting the balls. 'I shall need this shot next week,' he said. 'We are sure to be fighting a wind up there at some time. Those of us who haven't grown up on seaside courses must be able to cope with it.'

The man assumed that I would know automatically what he was talking about, so fully it occupied his thoughts. It took me a second or two to realise that he was referring to the Open championship at Muirfield in Scotland. I had forgotten for the moment that the great contest was now so imminent, but this would seem so like sacrilege to Bullimore that I did not confess it. Instead I said bemusedly, 'You seem to be hitting the ball very long without a great deal of effort, Alfred.'

This obviously pleased him. 'It is the coming method, John. The days of slashing at the ball with savage energy are almost over, though no doubt I shall find some of the older men and the amateurs lunging as hard as ever up in Edinburgh. But you must swing the club, not hit at the ball. Harry Vardon says so, and I am content to follow the man I consider the greatest golfer of our age. Indeed, I labour daily to implement his methods. Perhaps next week I shall show the great man that I have learned them well enough to surpass even him – he will be teaching his members today, you see, whilst I am free to practise, to make myself ready for the great event. In that respect at least, I have the advantage of him!'

He commenced hitting balls again towards the distant green, pausing only to register the behaviour in flight of each one, to watch its distant bounce towards the others he had hit before it. I watched him for a moment, impressed despite myself by the beauty of his striking, by the rhythm of his broad shoulders as they turned back and down through his swing. Then I looked round this deserted area and was irritated anew by his brazen disregard for his personal safety. There were clumps of furze and copses of birch trees all around him, as well as taller trees at a little greater distance. If he had been looking for a spot where he might be attacked, he could scarcely have selected a better one.

'Have you no consideration for your personal safety at

all?' I said eventually as he continued to hit balls and ignore me. I fear that in my exasperation it emerged almost as a shout. A pair of thrushes rose in alarm from the neighbouring brake and flapped away over our heads. 'There have already been two attempts on your life and yet you deliberately isolate yourself out here! If you have to practise, you bone-headed idiot, why do you not at least do it in the neighbourhood of the clubhouse, where anyone creeping near to you would be likely to be seen by others?'

As if to reinforce my point, a low, scudding rain began to sweep across the deserted course at that moment. Bullimore looked round him bemusedly, as if he registered now for the first time the danger he might be in. 'I have to practise,' he said stubbornly. 'I am using the holes we designate as suitable practice areas for our members. The Secretary cannot be a law unto himself, you know. He must observe the rules we lay down for others.'

'Even in these circumstances?' I said. 'Come, Alfred, you are being courageous to the point of foolishness, and a moment's thought will tell you that.'

'I came here to practise hitting balls into a north-west wind. I need to do that as part of my preparation. This rain could be a bonus: we are very likely to have to contend with conditions like this on at least one day next week.' And he began to hit balls through the low clouds of sweeping drizzle with renewed vigour.

That was why he had come here: to get the conditions he wanted. It was nothing to do with using the designated practice areas. It was another example of his reckless disregard for the danger which surrounded him, of the obsession with his golf which overrode all prudence. 'If you cannot be persuaded to exercise any sensible precautions, I have not the patience to advise you any further!' I said angrily, and I stalked away and left him to it.

I looked back as I walked past the tee of the hole to where he stood eighty yards away, an isolated, ferociously dedicated figure, hitting golf balls through wind and rain, silhouetted against a bleak grey sky.

TEN

It was another five days before Holmes returned. He looked drawn and exhausted, and I guessed he had not been eating properly as events developed towards a climax up in Westmoreland. He told me the story of the case on that Tuesday night, but it has no connection with this narrative, save that it removed him from it at a vital time, and I shall not digress into it here. I sent him off to bed whilst I made a few notes on what he had told me, as a skeleton for a future account of the affair.

I delved eagerly into the pages of *The Times* on Thursday morning, for I knew that the scores from the first day of the Open championship would be in the sports columns. Alfred Bullimore might be a pig-headed fool, where his own safety was concerned, but I still wanted to see how he was faring up in Muirfield. Indeed, his dedication to the game at the expense of every other consideration in life compelled a reluctant admiration in me for this singular fellow. It certainly increased my interest in how he was progressing in what he plainly regarded as the greatest week of his life.

I was not disappointed. I read that the weather had been kind to the golfers assembled in Muirfield for this greatest of all the game's contests; that the field numbered sixty-four golfers in all, the vast majority of them professionals; that the great J.H. Taylor and Harry Vardon had taken huge crowds of enthusiastic Scots round the course with them as they began the contest; and last but not least, that Alfred Bullimore, the leading amateur in the field, was lying just two shots behind the leader after a first round of 79.

Holmes appeared late but seemingly refreshed by a good night's sleep. He waved away the over-solicitous Mrs Hudson but ate an excellent breakfast. I told him enthusiastically of our man's progress in the Open. He did not seem very interested, but his attitude was abruptly transformed when I recounted to him the dramatic events at Sandwich of a fortnight earlier. He watched me as though under a spell as I recounted the story of the shooting of the unfortunate George Jackson.

'You inspected the scene of the shooting?'

'Indeed I did, Holmes. As a matter of fact, I was able to pinpoint the very spot where Jackson fell by means of the close observation you might have applied yourself. I found a small bloodstain which I am quite sure had come from poor Jackson's veins.'

'He was shot from behind, you say. At what range?'

'That I cannot be sure of. Nor, I fancy, could anyone else. Had you been in that cobbled alley, you would have seen how little there was to discover.' I was a little put out that he did not compliment me on either my dedication in rushing so promptly to the area or my diligence in applying his methods, but Holmes had never much time for the courtesies when his interest was aroused.

'You discovered nothing at the scene of this crime?'

'On the contrary, Holmes, I found something that you may think of great interest. Something the police officers seemed to have missed.' I smiled at him, then went over to my tobacco jar on the mantelpiece. I confess that I felt rather like a stage magician as I produced the twist of paper from within it and handed it to my friend.

He unwrapped it impatiently. 'A cartridge case. You found this at the scene of the crime?'

I nodded proudly. 'Some fifteen yards beyond the point where Jackson was shot, to be precise. It was embedded in the wall at the end of the alley. It's my belief –'

But Holmes had sprung up and raced to his desk and his microscope. 'A .22 bullet. From a pistol, I'm sure of it!' He delved into the drawer in his desk and produced a distorted brass cylinder, very similar to the one I had given him. 'Fired from the same pistol as this one: I'd put my life on that!'

I looked at him in amazement. 'Where did you get that cartridge, Holmes?'

'Why, from an oak tree exactly ten yards from where Bullimore was shot at Blackheath. I prised it out of the wood with your penknife.'

'Then why did you not reveal it at the time?'

He shrugged, as though contemplating the matter for the first time. 'It was of no relevance then. And there was no point in letting our man know that we had found this evidence. You must see that if he had known that I had discovered this, he would scarcely have used the same weapon again and thus linked the two shootings so firmly for us. Now, Watson, tell me again the full story of your trip to Sandwich and of the events which prompted it.'

Patiently, I told him again the details of it; of how George Jackson had been the only man in a large field who had duplicated Bullimore's choice of distinctive light green tweed clothing; of how easy it would have been to mistake the two identically dressed men for each other as darkness descended upon the St George's Club at Sandwich; of how the unsuspecting Bullimore had left for his hotel in a closed brougham, thus very possibly saving his own life; of how the unidentified assailant had followed the wrong quarry through the darkness and shot him down from behind.

'I should have known of this earlier.' Holmes stroked a finger down his long nose.

'It is scarcely my fault that you did not. You left us no address where I could get word to you of what had happened. In any case, I flatter myself that had you been there, you could have achieved no more than I did.'

'If you really want my opinion, Watson, I think that had I been in Sandwich, I should now have brought this case to its only possible conclusion.'

'And I am confident that had you been there you would have come no nearer to discovering the man or woman who is bent on killing Alfred Bullimore than I did!'

I stood facing him by his desk, breathing heavily. I did not see how he could possibly claim to be so near to a solution of this baffling saga. Yet I knew from previous experience that he was not given to empty boasts. Something nagged at me, saying that after all I must have missed something vital, that Holmes's assertion was more than mere vanity.

I glared at him, challenging him to justify himself, but he was busy contemplating the two cartridge cases under his microscope. Without looking up, he said, 'You had better get out the *Bradshaw*, Watson. We need to get a train down to Sandwich, as quickly as possible.'

I fumed inwardly at his cavalier treatment, but I did as I was bid. His attitude told me that there was need for haste, though I could not for the life of me fathom why. We were in the hansom and on the way to the station before I brought myself to speak to him again. 'Well at least Bullimore is still alive, despite your reluctance to take my advice and bring the police in at Blackheath. It is a mercy for you that the attacker at Sandwich chose the wrong man.'

'On the contrary, Watson, it is the fact that the attacker turned his pistol upon the wrong man which makes our journey today of such extreme urgency.'

ELEVEN

The train drew into Sandwich station with a hissing exhalation of steam and a whistle of brakes as the small tanker engine stopped just short of the buffers. It was a quarter to two and Holmes had repeatedly looked at his hunter as the last section of the journey tried his patience. I could not see the reason for his haste, nor what he could find here that I had not already discovered. But I saw his chin thrust deep into his chest and his sunken eyes staring unseeingly through the window of the carriage, and I knew better than to interrupt his thoughts.

'Do you want to trace the route George Jackson took from the golf club, or shall I take you straight to the scene of the shooting?' I said.

He came out of his reverie with my question. 'What? Oh no, Watson. There is nothing more to be discovered in either of those places. I believe you found whatever was to be found there. I have no doubt that your observation was first class; it is your deductions that were imperfect. If we find what I fear we shall find, we shall then have to move quickly if we are to avoid further bloodshed. There is a madness at work in this business, as we agreed months ago. I had not thought it would take so dangerous a turn.'

When we came out of the station, he turned not towards

the golf club, nor towards the place where George Jackson had lodged, but into the quaint old town, with its narrow, winding streets and bow-fronted shops. There was not much of it, and only one shop of the kind Holmes was looking for. The man behind the long counter was disappointed with our enquiry, for he had anticipated a sale to one or both of us. It took Holmes a few seconds to convince him of the importance of his peremptory questions, but he eventually called his assistant out from the rear rooms, and they compared notes about all purchases in the previous week. There was none of the kind we sought.

Holmes thrust his hands deep into the pockets of his jacket as we stood in the cobbled street outside. 'There is a kind of cunning in this madness; our assassin does what he can to cover his tracks, despite his overweening arrogance in what he plans. I should have known he would not shop so close to home for what he needed.'

He decided we should split our efforts in the interests of discovering speedily the evidence he needed. He briefed me on what I must do, and I knew better than to question the reasons for it at this stage. As Holmes took on the appropriate establishments in Broadstairs, I went round the shops in Ramsgate with the strange set of enquiries I had heard him put to the man in Sandwich. Both of us drew blanks. Holmes was by this time near distraction in his frustration. As we careered south along the coast in a cab I feared would come off the winding road – Holmes had offered the driver an extra guinea if he covered the twelve miles in record time – he muttered to himself, 'It must be so, it cannot be else! There is no other explanation which will fit the facts!'

For my part, I was still doubtful whether we would find the evidence he required. And even if we did, I was still more at a loss to see how George Jackson's vanity, his indulgence of a sartorial whim, could possibly be at the root of this strange sequence of events.

We found what we wanted in a small shop in a lane behind the seafront at Deal. We could easily have missed the narrow front of the place, but it was the only gents' outfitter in the place, and we were accurately directed to it by a man flinging a ball for his terrier in the brisk sea-winds which swept across the beach.

The proprietor, Mr Peebles, was an elderly but still dapper man, with a modestly rounded waistcoat giving him an appropriate gravity and pince-nez spectacles on the end of his small nose. He looked as though it was a long time since he had been addressed as peremptorily as he now was by Holmes, but he had the information we wanted and he did not hesitate over the delivery of it. He worked alone in the small shop; trade did not justify a regular assistant, especially during the winter months. He could have remembered much smaller purchases than the one which interested us, had it been necessary.

A gentleman had indeed purchased a distinctive light green tweed suit on the Tuesday of the previous week. Not made to measure, which was unusual, but not unique. Indeed, when Mr Peebles had offered his bespoke tailoring service, the customer waved it aside, saying that his need was too urgent and his time too limited to attend for the necessary fittings. He had taken the suit away in a brown paper parcel that evening; our informant remembered it vividly because he had taken up the cuffs whilst his customer strolled impatiently along the seafront. It had made Mr Peebles late closing and late home for his supper, events plainly so rare that they were etched upon his memory.

Holmes drew a long breath, then exhaled slowly. It was a strange sound, compounded partly of satisfaction, partly of relief, and partly of excitement for what must now follow. Now, at last, he might reveal his thinking to me. I said, 'We have tracked it down at last then, this strange purchase. I still don't see its significance. So George Jackson saw the distinctive suit that Alfred was wearing and rather fancied a similar outfit for himself. It is a little garish, to my mind, but there's no accounting for taste. The fact that he rushed here to purchase a suit in the same tweed may account for his injuries, I can see that. He could easily have been mistaken for Alfred when they were the only two in the field wearing that distinctive apparel. But I had already deduced that and reported it to you. There was scarcely need for today's wild perambulations in search of this purchase to document it!'

'You think not, Watson? Yes, still you think not – I see it in your face! Then I must tell you why we have spent the day as we have. It was necessary for us to find this place not to register the purchase in our notes, but the purchaser.'

'But I can't for the life of me see why it was necessary to prove that poor George Jackson –'

But Holmes had turned impatiently away from me to the bewildered outfitter. 'Describe the man who bought this green tweed suit, please, Mr Peebles.'

The Pickwickian figure with the tape measure round his neck thought for a moment; he was not a man for haste. 'An impatient kind of fellow. Thick-set chap, middle thirties, I should think, but very fit. He had a big moustache.'

I looked at Sherlock Holmes, who permitted himself a tiny smile at my discomfiture before I said, 'Alfred Bullimore! But why, Holmes? I had thought –'

'There is no time now, Watson. You will work it out in due course for yourself, I am sure. But where is Bullimore at this moment? We must go to him.'

'That's easy, Holmes. I told you, but you did not heed me in your anxiety to come here. He is playing in the Open Championship.'

Those grey eyes I knew so well opened wide in horror. 'That is the greatest of all golfing competitions, is it not?'

'Indeed it is, Holmes. It has been Alfred's ultimate goal for the whole of the year. He has been gearing his whole life to it, indeed.'

'And where is this competition taking place?'

'It could scarcely be further away from where we stand on the south coast, Holmes. You told me the venue yourself, many weeks ago. The Open is being held this year at Muirfield in Scotland. The best part of five hundred miles north of here.'

'And Bullimore qualified for the final stages?'

'I am happy to tell you that he not only qualified, Holmes, but is doing exceptionally well. He is holding his own against the finest professionals in the land. Indeed, when I last read of his exploits, before you rushed me down here, Alfred was lying but two strokes behind the leader of the competition after the first round.'

Holmes's face filled not with excitement but with horror. 'This was yesterday?'

'Yes. They play the second round today, and the final two rounds tomorrow. I'm looking forward to finding how Alfred has fared today. I shall –'

But Holmes was ahead of me, racing out into the quiet streets of Deal, stopping the news-vendor's shout before it began as he thrust his coin urgently into the grubby hand. He pushed the evening paper into my hands. 'Here. You know where to find the scores. Check it. Quickly, for God's sake!'

Some of his excitement had passed like an electric current into me as our hands briefly touched. I saw my fingers trembling as they turned the pages, too slowly, too clumsily. There was a brief account of the golf above the morning scores from Muirfield. But I had to turn to the stop press before I found the information I wanted. 'Alfred is doing well still!' I called excitedly. 'He is two shots away from the leader after the second round, and there is only one famous name ahead of him now. That is the great Harry Vardon.'

Instead of being excited by our friend's dizzy progress, Holmes sprang away in horror, racing to the tiny station. 'We must get to London quickly, Watson! Quickly enough to catch the night train to Edinburgh and to Muirfield.'

'Come, Holmes, the matter cannot be as urgent as that. Mrs Hudson will be expecting us back for dinner, and we need to pack the correct –'

He was at the station ticket office now as he shouted over his shoulder, 'We must catch the night train, Watson. Surely you see now that it is our only chance to avoid bloodshed, perhaps even murder!'

TWELVE

We caught the night train from King's Cross, but only just.

The porters were slamming the carriage doors and the huge engine giving its preliminary long snort of steam as we raced through the ticket barrier and on to the platform. Even as we tumbled through the last open door, the guard waved his green flag above his head and shrilled his whistle, and the great locomotive eased its long line of carriages slowly forward with the first of a series of mighty explosions of smoke beneath the high roof of the station.

We had a first-class compartment to ourselves, and the softly sprung seats were very comfortable. It had been a long and hectic day and the rhythm of the wheels as we settled eventually to a steady speed was quite soporific. I do not know whether Holmes slept or not. My last memory of him that night was of that gaunt profile staring tensely out into the night as the great train rumbled northwards. Then I fell into what was at first an uneasy doze, for I was still not clear about Holmes's thinking and still deeply anxious about the threat to my friend Alfred Bullimore.

Waking with a start and finding Holmes still staring tense and unseeing at a window now swimming with rain, I looked at my pocket watch and found that Thursday had passed into Friday. I pulled the window blind down on my side of the carriage and sank more deeply into the folds of my Ulster. I had trained myself whilst on active service in India to sleep in all kinds of situations, and found it a valuable, indeed a necessary, attribute. At around one a.m., I fell into a deeper sleep. I remember stirring briefly as the train strained up over the Cheviots – I think we enlisted the help of an extra engine for the long, steep incline there – but by the time I became fully aware of my surroundings, it was daylight and we were running into the suburbs of Edinburgh.

And still Holmes sat as I had seen him on the previous evening. He might have stretched his long legs out a little further and sunk a fraction lower into his cape, but his gaze through the window towards the approaching city was as unblinking as ever. His intensity seemed to have made the grey eyes sink even deeper into the hollows above the sallow cheeks. Long before we drew level with the long flagged platform of the station, he had pulled the deer-stalker down over his ears, clearly impatient for action after the long night of tense anticipation.

Neither Holmes nor I had ever been to Muirfield. Although it was famous as the home of 'The Honourable Company of Edinburgh Golfers', we found on enquiry that the links was a good twenty miles and more from the centre of the city. We had to squeeze on to a local train, crowded even at that early hour with Scottish golfing enthusiasts, carrying copious solid and liquid refreshments out to the course where they would become part of the greatest golfing day of the year. It was the multitude of Scottish voices, soft and harsh by turns according to where they had begun their pilgrimage to this golfing Mecca, which swiftly made us aware that this was the last day of the Open championship, where the finest golfers of all fought out the contest, over thirty-six holes, on a great and spectacular links.

They were a good-humoured lot, our companions, united despite a wide range of backgrounds by their anticipation of a fine day's sport. There was support for their local heroes, some of whom were known to them personally, but the general consensus was that the great Englishmen, Harry Vardon and J.H. Taylor (he was universally known by his initials, and no one in the crowded carriage was sure of his Christian names), would take some stopping, especially now, when they had played the two rounds on Wednesday and Thursday well, and were moving into the last day with most of their rivals already behind them.

I did not catch everything in these strange accents, especially the repartee: often I found myself smiling in sympathy, rather than understanding, as the carriage dissolved into raucous laughter at some trenchant golfing comment. But I kept my ears alert for any mention of my friend's chances. It was not until someone raised the prospect of an amateur winning that I heard Alfred's name mentioned. Then one of the men who had been present during the second round on the previous day spoke of how doughtily he had performed; he classed him as a 'braw strong hitter' and spoke of how he had flighted his ball low through the wind 'as well as any paid man'. I was almost moved to declare my acquaintance, for had I not seen him practising those very shots when we last met? But something in Holmes's gaunt and rigid profile made me hold my peace, and the packed little train eventually ran into the tiny station without either of us having spoken a word.

Holmes asked me a question as we were swept through the ticket barrier on the grey-green tide of cloth caps. It was the first time in ten hours that he had uttered more than a monosyllable, and from a man not given to melodrama, it was much to the point. 'You have your service revolver, Watson?' he asked.

He knew I had, for I had carried it with me on my first visit to Sandwich, after the shooting of George Jackson, and I was determined to offer Alfred Bullimore whatever protection I could now, when the villain who was out to kill him would surely not make such a mistake again. I said softly, 'I have it loaded, with the safety catch on, in the inside pocket of my overcoat.' The fact that Holmes bothered to check what he already knew was so warned me that he was on edge; I began to feel that before this day was out we should have either a death or a resolution of this affair. But not both, please God not both, I found myself praying silently.

'You had better find where your man is, and quickly,' said Holmes, as we entered a golf course that was already surprisingly dense with spectators.

I had never been to an Open before. I had a vague idea that the players would go off in the order of their scores, with the leaders last, reversing the neat order of the scores as they appeared in the morning papers. But there was no such logic; the competitors left the tee in the order in which they were drawn, I was told sternly by the official in the scorer's hut, this being thought the fairest method of ensuring that no golfer had an unfair advantage.

This meant that Alfred might be anywhere, for it was now just after nine o'clock, and the golf had commenced at eight. I rushed to the first tee, locating it by the warm applause which had greeted a good drive from the latest competitor to strike off. From the starter there, I found that Alfred was already on the course: he had begun his round at eight-thirty.

I raced back to my appointed meeting place with Holmes, in front of the main door of the clubhouse. 'He is already on the course and in danger,' I called breathlessly. 'We must get to him quickly if we are to be of any use as protection. The starter says he will be on the fourth green, or thereabouts. We shall find him easily enough, he says, for there will be a great crowd following the match behind him, because Harry Vardon is playing in that. Come, there is no time to lose!'

'On the contrary, Watson, this is excellent news. We shall have breakfast, I think, after all.' And to my astonishment, Holmes led us off the course and into the nearby Marine Hotel, where he ordered a huge breakfast for both of us and proceeded to do it full, leisurely justice. Then he lit a pipe and filled our corner of the hotel lounge with pungent clouds of the strongest of his tobaccos. 'It is the Scottish mixture, Watson,' he said as I protested. 'Perhaps I shall be able to replenish my stocks before we get the train home – I believe my supplier is in the centre of Edinburgh.'

It was now approaching half past ten. I said, 'Really Holmes, this is too much! You came here in such haste that I had to send a telegram to Mrs Hudson to inform her of our movements, and now we apparently have all the time in the world.'

'Not all the time in the world, Watson, no. That is in any case a curiously meaningless expression, I always think. But time enough, with our man on the course. But come! You have, I know, a certain interest in this game. Let us go and see how your man is progressing. Let us watch him like two hungry hawks as he concludes his morning round.' And with that, my friend sprang suddenly to his feet and moved swiftly out through the hall to the exit doors of the hotel.

These sudden changes of mood had long since ceased to surprise me. In retrospect, I can see that this leisurely interlude at the Marine Hotel was the calm before the storm. Holmes had the capacity of many active men to take full advantage of periods of rest; he had been nervous through the night, but he now knew as I did not that the outrage he had raced here to prevent could not happen during this morning period. I wish he had explained as much to me, but that was never his way of doing things.

Holmes now asked me to point out the places where the golfers changed and took lunch. The professionals were not in 1896 allowed into the clubhouse, but there was a shed nearby where they changed. If I knew Alfred Bullimore, he would have based himself in there with them, as he had at Sandwich. He believed all golfers were equal on the course and elsewhere, he said, when competing, and I admired the spirit in which he carried this idea through in his own conduct. For a moment, Holmes studied the geography of the area, which was busy with golfers and their caddies. Then, acknowledging my mounting impatience, he conceded at last that we might now seek out our man on the course.

We found Alfred quickly enough by using the method

the starter had suggested to me earlier in the morning. We sought out the huge crowd following the fortunes of Harry Vardon, probably the most famous of all the illustrious golfers in the field. He was on the fifteenth, and the huge crowd made a natural amphitheatre of the green. He chipped expertly up to the flag as we arrived, leaving his ball within a foot of it, and there was a roar of approval from his following. No doubt these Scots would have preferred the man to be one of their own, but they were knowledgeable and appreciative about this game so many of them played, and they relished the smooth skills of this man who was doing so much to popularise the game.

I spotted Alfred Bullimore on the hole in front of Vardon's match, just as the starter had told me I would. He and his companion were carrying with them their own, much smaller gallery, and there was a round of applause as we approached, when Alfred holed a curling seven-foot putt. His nerve was holding in the crisis, I told Holmes with satisfaction. My companion said gnomically that that might or might not be a good thing. I could not understand this, but I put it down to the fact that Holmes knew nothing about golf, whereas I felt myself by this time to be something of an expert, after the last four months.

By comparing notes with other spectators whilst the players walked up the fairway after their drives at the seventeenth, I found that Alfred's companion was well out of it, being now some fifteen strokes behind the best men, but that Alfred was hanging on well, keeping in contact with the leader even while other great names down the field were falling away. This time I could not resist declaring my personal connection. 'Alfred is a fine golfer,' I said. 'I have played with him myself, and had close contact with him over the last few weeks. He has prepared himself well for this. I do not think he will collapse easily, even if things get tight in the last round this afternoon.'

Holmes heard something of this exchange; I caught him looking at me disapprovingly, but he said nothing, and my new companion and I continued to exchange notes on what was happening on the rest of the course. I said nothing of Alfred's obsession with the game, which seemed now almost justified as he mounted his challenge for the greatest prize of all. Indeed, in the heady atmosphere of the last day of the Open at Muirfield, when we heard cheers from all parts of the course for the remarkable feats being achieved, I doubt whether the dedicated Scots around me would have even understood the idea that a man could give too much devotion to this ancient game.

It was an invigorating morning for those watching, though the scores throughout that day showed how tricky the conditions were for golf. There had been blustery showers earlier, while we were enjoying our princely breakfast, but now the sun shone and provided some warmth to counteract the stiff breeze which gusted in over the Firth of Forth. I was glad to see Alfred was back in the russet tweeds I had come to think of as his golfing uniform; presumably he had abandoned the light green suit after the unfortunate shooting at Sandwich, which had cost George Jackson his chance to appear in this great arena.

He made a solid four at the seventeenth, then hit a marvellous brassie shot from the centre of the fairway at the eighteenth, and pitched his niblick through a strong cross-wind to within fifteen feet of the hole. His gallery was increasing all the time with the news of his brave scoring in the testing conditions, and many more now strolled out of the clubhouse to see him complete his round; I think the members were excited by the prospect of an amateur holding his own against the established professionals.

I was waiting to see how Alfred fared with his putting on the last green when a strong hand gripped my forearm. 'Take these, Watson.' Holmes handed me his cape and his deerstalker hat. 'And stick close to your man when he finishes his round!'

He was gone before I could question him, his long legs carrying him swiftly over the rough ground, his movements full of urgency now after the lethargy he had displayed an hour ago. I felt my pulses racing as he disappeared from my sight. The crisis could surely not now be long delayed. I checked for the fourth time since we had arrived to follow Bullimore on the course that my revolver was ready for use in the inside pocket of my Ulster.

Alfred did not hole his first putt on the eighteenth, but he left it within six inches of the hole, then knocked in the short one to a roar of appreciation from the crowd for his achievement. He looked drained by his efforts, and I decided not to come forward from the crowd to congratulate him as I had intended. It would be better if nothing distracted him now, for he must snatch a hasty lunch and present himself at the first tee within an hour for the last round of the competition. But I would follow him closely; if Holmes said he needed protection now, then this must surely be the crucial time.

Alfred signed his score card and handed it in at the

scorer's shed. There was a huge crowd around the spot, as there were no scoreboards on the course and the only news of how the whole field was faring was the sheet of scores the officials pinned to the outer side of their shed, bringing things up to date with a new sheet every twenty minutes or so. Alfred was soon elated. He emerged from the shed looking a new man, with the news of how the scoring was going. His eighty in that wind meant he had more than held his own when others around him were falling by the wayside. J.H. Taylor was out late and still had much of his round to play. Of the others, only Harry Vardon, who had played immediately behind Alfred and matched him almost stroke for stroke, was ahead of him. It seemed almost certain that Alfred would lie second at lunch when all had completed their morning rounds, a mere two strokes behind the great Vardon.

I looked round anxiously for Holmes to relay the great news, but he was nowhere to be seen. I could not afford to be distracted, for it was my mission to remain close to Alfred throughout this dangerous lunchtime period, when the crowds which could contain his mysterious assailant might surge close around him.

Alfred Bullimore said with relish to his caddy, 'That is the first part of the job done, Bob. Away and get yourself something to eat, and take the clubs with you.' The man touched his cap and hurried away to join the queue at the pie-stall in front of the Marine Hotel. There was no special provision for caddies, but some of the spectators pushed him forward in the queue when they saw that he was carrying clubs for one of the gladiators of this great day.

I followed closely behind Alfred Bullimore, trying to

keep a watch for anyone who might be planning mischief towards him in the swirling crowds around the clubhouse. It was a near-impossible task in the throng, but I kept my hand on my service revolver, which I had now transferred to the side pocket of my coat. I was glad that I had not made myself known to him, for it would have been even more difficult to protect him if I had been at his side and engaged in any sort of conversation.

As I had anticipated, he went into the large shed which had been set aside as changing facilities for the professional competitors. This building was strictly reserved for the golfers, and a steward on the door ensured that I could not follow Alfred through it. But I consoled myself with the thought that he was probably much safer in that quiet place with his fellow-golfers than he was outside it, in the cosmopolitan throngs which moved around this busy area.

That thought was reinforced by the arrival immediately after Alfred of Harry Vardon, who had now finished his round in the match after Alfred. His vociferous supporters accompanied him to the very door of the changing-room, where they were firmly barred by the steward. They were a good-natured lot, quickly accepting the idea that their man needed a period of quiet for rest and refreshment if he was to give of his best in the final round of the great contest. They melted away amid joking and laughter, arranging their meeting-places for the final act of the great pageant in the afternoon.

Vardon was not in the shed for very long; he emerged after no more than three minutes. By this time, I was becoming a little anxious about the whereabouts of my man, but Alfred emerged immediately after the great golfer who was leading the competition and followed him round the side of the shed, beneath an arrow which was accompanied by the hand-written notice, 'Refreshments for Competitors Only'.

I followed at about five yards' distance, determined now to keep Alfred in my sight for the rest of the interval between rounds, if possible. I was aware as I did so of a ragged figure at my side: a caddie perhaps, but I was too anxious to keep my eye on the disappearing Bullimore to give him much immediate attention. I followed Vardon and Alfred down the side of the large shed, and found myself in a narrow, deserted passage between the back of the shed and a large tent, which presumably contained the promised refreshments for the golfers.

The next events happened so quickly that it took me some minutes to realise fully just what had happened. A voice from the ragged figure at my side whispered urgently, 'The pistol, Watson, if you please!' and I realised with a shock that the untidy figure beside me was none other than Sherlock Holmes. At the same moment as I passed my revolver limply into his hand, I was horrified to see Alfred Bullimore draw a pistol from the pocket of his jacket and aim it at the unsuspecting Harry Vardon, who was stepping over the guy rope of the tent beside him, no more than five paces ahead. I know I shouted, but I do not remember to this day what the words were. I think it was a warning to Vardon, and an injunction to Holmes to fire himself, to protect the innocent master-golfer. I do remember vividly what happened next in that narrow passage between shed and tent: Bullimore pressed the trigger of his pistol, and Holmes did not press his.

But there was no sudden loud report of gunfire, no sinking of a stricken Vardon ahead of us. Bullimore pressed the trigger once, twice, three times in rapid succession, then stood looking stupidly down at the weapon. Then Holmes's voice cracked out behind him, sharp as the gunfire he had failed to produce. 'You had better give that pistol to Dr Watson now, I think. It is quite useless to you, you see: the ammunition you thought was in its chambers is here.' Holmes opened the fingers of his left hand, revealing the cartridges Bullimore had sought to fire into the unsuspecting Harry Vardon, poised now like a horrified statue ahead of us. 'On the other hand, the weapon in my hand is very much loaded, and I do not advise you to test the truth of that.'

Bullimore did not attempt escape. We led him, with head cast down and those great shoulders slumped, round the side of the shed to the two constables Holmes had asked to await us there. They completed the formalities of the arrest and led him away to a Black Maria in the streets of the little village of Gullane.

Harry Vardon, who could still scarcely believe that he had been so near to injury or death, ate a hasty sandwich and was back on the first tee by his appointed time of twelve-forty. Vast and noisy throngs followed the excitements of the last round of the Open of 1896. Very few of them knew anything of the dramatic events which had evolved in the hour before it commenced.

THIRTEEN

We had a carriage to ourselves for the long journey back to London. Holmes, relaxed now with the case concluded and an excellent dinner inside him, produced his briar pipe and stretched his long legs contentedly across the first-class compartment. 'I shall sleep, I think, on the journey south,' he said.

'Not yet you won't!' I said firmly. I've pieced together a little of this. I realise that you adopted your caddie's role again this afternoon to gain entry to the changing shed and remove the ammunition from Bullimore's pistol. But how on earth you worked out that Bullimore himself was at the bottom of all this I simply can't see. Why on earth should he come and ask us to investigate the matter, if he himself was the culprit?'

'Arrogance, I fear, Watson. Despite your sensational accounts of my earlier successes, Bullimore thought he could outwit us. No doubt he thought as I do that the powers you attribute to me in your reports are much exaggerated.'

'Well, he certainly succeeded in outwitting me,' I said ruefully. 'But why come to us at all, if he wished his villainy to go undetected?'

'Because he was arrogant, as I say, and also a little mad. The police were bound to be involved, when he moved on to serious villainy. He thought he could divert any suspicion from himself by invoking the services of Sherlock Holmes and making himself the apparent victim of the earlier and less serious offences. He was confident apparently that I would not see through his shoddy little deceptions. But you, Watson, were the one who spotted the lunacy. Because you were a golfer as I am not, you saw much more of him at close quarters in the area which obsessed him.'

'But I thought it no more than a tiresome devotion to a sport, at the expense of all else, including his relationships with people. I had not realised the full danger in it.'

'He obviously didn't recognise the transition from dedication into madness himself. Eventually even human life could not be allowed to stand between him and his goals in the sport. He removed George Jackson from the tournament at Sandwich. It was only when I heard of that that I realised we had to take his obsession seriously, as a threat to other lives. I divined that the shooting at Blackheath had been contrived, but I had no notion at that time that he would turn his weapon upon others.'

'But you imply that you suspected Bullimore from the start. I don't see how you could have done.'

'There were certain pointers. All the evidence he brought to us on that first morning in Baker Street revolved around him and him alone. He was the only witness to most of the things which had happened. He told us that morning that the earlier messages had come through the post, but Mrs Ross told us later that all the threatening letters had been hand-delivered. Yet no one had seen any of them arrive. Nor had he kept any of them for our perusal, as he would surely have done if they had disturbed him as much as he claimed. Even the message he did produce for us on that first visit had been left on the course where he would find it, according to him. In a hut where people went only to shelter from the rain, he said. Yet he came to us on a fine bright morning; why should he ever have gone into the hut in those circumstances?'

'But I thought the implication was that the letter-writer was someone who knew the Secretary's every movement about the club, who could place things where he alone would find them.'

'That is what he wanted us to believe, certainly. The alternative explanation was that the events had been contrived by the person at the centre of them, for his own ends. One has to be alive to all the possibilities of every situation, Watson. Observation and deduction, as always, are the twin pillars of detection. But having observed, you must be alive to all possible deductions. Then, as more facts emerge, only one of several alternative original deductions will remain possible. That is what happened in this case.' He began to fill his pipe, slowly, methodically and with great contentment. I had an uneasy feeling that he was pacing his smoking preparations to accompany his explanation, for he was clearly enjoying my questions.

'And you felt this from the start?'

Holmes considered the matter, looking out at the dramatic outline of the Cheviot Hills against a setting sun. 'No. I felt it was a possibility that things were not as Bullimore put them to us, that was all. When we visited the club at Blackheath the next day, I became increasingly certain of it.'

'That is when you practised your deception on me and acted as my caddie.'

'Aye lad. "Ye could become a gey wee golfer with a wee bit o' practice, and the right man on the bag!"' He dropped easily into the soft Scottish accent he had used that day, and with his grin I caught a rare glimpse of the schoolboy he must once have been. 'But you may remember that I said at the time that I found it "quite instructive" watching Alfred Bullimore on the golf course. I didn't mean his golf, Watson, but his bearing. He had told us on the previous day, "I have an uncomfortable feeling that I am being watched, both on and off the golf course". Yet he seemed remarkably relaxed, playing his best golf, concentrating as only a man at ease can do.'

'That was certainly so. I put it down merely to his obsession with the game. But you're right that he should have been more scared – even two weeks later when he was shot, he didn't seem as upset as he should have been.'

'No. His chief anxiety on the day after that shooting seemed to be that we should not inform the police about the attack. In my experience, Watson, people who have been attacked in that way are only too anxious to bring the police into the matter immediately. You told him quite bluntly that he was being arrogant in not contacting the police: the truth is that Bullimore did not want them involved because he felt in no danger: the only injury he had suffered was self-inflicted. He wanted to make himself seem the target rather than the perpetrator of this incident, because of what he might need to do to his golfing rivals in the months to come. I should have realised the danger to them at the time – especially in the light of the injuries done to old Captain Osborne and his dog. People who are prepared to ill-treat animals and the elderly often move on to greater violence. I thought like you that Bullimore was merely in the grip of a harmless excess of zeal for the game. It was Mrs Christobel Ross, the person who knew his mind better than anyone, who gave us what should have been the pointer to that danger.'

I thought hard for a moment about the interviews we had conducted in that hot, dark room at the back of the Blackheath clubhouse. 'I remember Mrs Ross saying that it was Alfred's passion for golf which had led him into this danger.'

Holmes smiled, contemplating his filled pipe, feeling no need to light it yet; I was sure now that he was thoroughly enjoying himself as the long train rattled south into the twilight. 'As always, Watson, you remember the words of an attractive woman with particular clarity. Mrs Ross meant of course that his obsession with the game had led him to expose himself recklessly to attack, but she was right in a different way. His passion for the game had upset his moral judgement: he was now determined to win at all costs, even if that meant he must remove the most serious of his rivals by force. And it was obvious when he took us to the scene of the supposed ambush that no one had stood at the spot where he claimed the assassin had fired on him. I pointed out as much to you at the time.'

'That you did not, Holmes! It is true that you said the absence of foot-marks there was significant, but you allowed me to think that a woman or a child might have stood beneath that fir tree.'

'No, Watson, you allowed yourself to think that. And

indeed it might have been a possibility, had it not been for the marks of the rabbits there. I recall distinctly that I told you at the time that the tracks of the rabbits in that gloomy spot where Bullimore claimed to have been ambushed might prove the most significant evidence of all.'

'Well, you might have done, I suppose,' I admitted churlishly, 'but I still don't see –'

'Come, Watson, you must surely see now. There were fresh indentations in the damp surface from rabbits' paws. That was conclusive: it meant that even the lightest of human beings who had stood on that ground must surely have left some trace. Clearly no one had stood at the spot from which Bullimore claimed his attacker had fired upon him.'

'And he wouldn't let me examine his wound.' I was by now feeling very foolish; all this evidence had been there for me to take up, as easily as my old friend had done.

'No. His reluctance to reveal the damage set me thinking as soon as we arrived at the scene. I'm sure that had we been able to examine the wound, we should have found it was inflicted at much closer quarters than he claimed. From no more than a few inches in fact, by himself.'

'So his lucky escape was not that at all. He was careful to make sure that he received no more than a flesh wound in his upper arm.'

'Exactly! He was back to practising his golf the next day. He should have kept away from it rather longer if he wished his deception to be convincing, but his obsession with improving his skills did not allow him that.'

'So when he claimed he was ambushed, he simply went out behind the clubhouse to that path between the trees on the edge of darkness and carefully shot himself through the flesh of his arm.'

'Yes. He chose the time and the place cleverly to make sure there were few people about, other than those he chose should answer his cries for help. That was another significant thing, of course. This mysterious attacker of his had to escape from there either past Bullimore and into the clubhouse – which he claimed he had not done – or past the groundsman's hut. Yet Bevan, who was in his hut at the time of the shooting, had seen no one go that way.'

'Was it because you already suspected all this that you were anxious to inspect the interior of Bullimore's house on that night?'

'Indeed yes. And Bullimore's home, as I suggested to you it might be at the time, was quite informative. There were no pictures of women or close friends there to suggest a life away from golf. The place, if you remember, was filled with golfing pictures and trophies. It reinforced the picture of a man in the grip of a sporting obsession.'

'But if you deduced all this at the time, why did you do nothing about it?'

'There, my old friend and recorder, is where I made my mistake. I could see that Alfred Bullimore had contrived this elaborate charade, but I could not yet see why. The question intrigued me, so much so that I let the situation develop as I should not have done in the hope of discovering what he was about. I hope you will record my error if you ever chronicle this sad affair, Watson: it will mitigate somewhat the character of superman you have imposed upon me elsewhere. At the time, I could not see the purpose of Bullimore's deception, because I did not realise the extent of his obsession; I did not see him as a danger to anyone but himself. It took the shooting of George Jackson at Sandwich to alert me to the danger, which as you know I did not hear about until well after the event.'

'And it was the purchase of that light green tweed suit which confirmed for you that Bullimore had been the perpetrator rather than the intended victim of that shooting. I see now why we had that frantic trawl round the outfitters of Kent yesterday, and our even more frantic journey north to Muirfield through the night!'

'Yes, Watson, our confirmation of Bullimore's guilt lay in the purchase of that suit. He gave you the impression that Jackson had followed him in fashion, had emulated his choice of cloth, and been mistaken for him as a result. In fact, Bullimore had noted on the first day of that championship that the best golfer in the field, the man he feared would rob him of his triumph on the final day, was wearing that distinctive light green tweed. He hastily acquired a similar outfit for himself and appeared in it on the day when Jackson was shot. It was easy for people to conclude as he hoped that he had been the intended victim of that shooting. I doubt whether he intended to kill Jackson, or he would hardly have fired two shots at his legs. But there is no knowing what he would have done to Harry Vardon today, with the greatest golfing prize of all at stake. Madness swells and violence gets bolder when it is not checked. Shakespeare, I believe, is full of that notion, but I concern myself merely with the more tawdry crimes of our own day.'

And on that thought, Sherlock Holmes pulled down the blind on the darkness outside the racing train, set down his pipe unsmoked on the seat beside him, and fell into an exhausted but contented sleep.

EPILOGUE

Harry Vardon won the Open championship of 1896 at Muirfield, after a tie with J.H. Taylor, another member of golf's 'great triumvirate' of the years around the turn of the century. Vardon beat Taylor in a thirty-six-hole play-off for the title.

Alfred Bullimore was tried and found guilty of Assault with a Firearm in September, 1896. He was sentenced to five years in prison, with hard labour. After three years of his sentence, he was transferred to an institution for the mentally insane, on the intercession of Dr J.H. Watson and Mr Edward Frobisher, lawyer and Secretary of Blackheath Golf Club.

Bullimore was released from the asylum in 1904. He never played serious golf again.